PENGUIN METRO READS
SIMPLY COMPLICATED

An English honours graduate from St Stephen's College, Shreya Prabhu Jindal currently teaches English in Vasant Valley School, Delhi.

She started writing in 2003, when, at age thirteen, she discovered fan fiction. She has continued to read and write fan fiction since, and enjoys it immensely.

Shreya has also dabbled in scriptwriting. In 2009 she co-scripted a short film, *Kuch Spice to Make It Meetha*, for MadMidaas Films. The film, which stars Purab Kohli and Nauheed Cyrusi, was an instant hit on YouTube when it was uploaded in February 2012.

Another Chance at Life was her debut novel.

You can contact Shreya at shreyasnook@gmail.com.

Also by the same author

Another Chance at Life

Simply
COMPLICATED

Shreya Prabhu Jindal

Penguin
metro reads

An imprint of Penguin Random House

PENGUIN METRO READS

USA | Canada | UK | Ireland | Australia
New Zealand | India | South Africa | China | Singapore

Penguin Metro Reads is part of the Penguin Random House group of companies
whose addresses can be found at global.penguinrandomhouse.com

Published by Penguin Random House India Pvt. Ltd
4th Floor, Capital Tower 1, MG Road,
Gurugram 122 002, Haryana, India

Penguin
Random House
India

First published in Penguin Metro Reads by Penguin Books India 2014

ISBN 9780143419501

Typeset in Elegant Garamond by R. Ajith Kumar, New Delhi

Printed at Repro India Limited

www.penguin.co.in

MIX
Paper from
responsible sources
FSC® C047271

This is a legitimate digitally printed version of the book and therefore might not
have certain extra finishing on the cover.

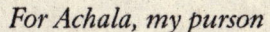

For Achala, my purson

ONE

When the first chords of 'Chop Suey' started playing on the speakers, Aastha Goyal smiled at her friend. 'Dude, this place is awesome!'

She wished more of her friends had agreed to come, but F-Bar was an expensive place and she had known not to be pushy.

'Told you you'd like it!' Sameer Mascarenas shouted over the music. 'We should come here more often.'

'Yeah, well, not all of us are able to afford it,' she reminded him. Unlike Sameer, who had started working immediately after college, she was still only halfway through her MA. She'd had to save a long time for this outing.

Sameer shrugged and began to scream out the lyrics of the song, his tall lean body swaying to the music. Aastha started swaying too, but kept her eyes on the crowd around her.

'Have you seen Paddy?' she asked.

'Nope. She's probably with Rahul.'

Aastha's smile faltered a little. She knew that Paddy was in the new-relationship honeymoon phase, but it was Aastha's birthday and she was her closest friend. Padmini should have been there, but she'd been so completely wrapped up in Rahul lately . . .

Sameer read her thoughts in a quick glance. 'Never mind,' he said. 'They'll probably show up soon. And in the meantime, am I not good enough company?'

Aastha rolled her eyes, deciding to dismiss the matter from her mind. Sameer was right—he was great company and she was having a good time with or without Paddy, which was all that mattered.

'Hey, do you want something to drink?' Sameer asked after a while.

'Sure,' she said. 'A mocktail, though. I can't afford any more alcohol.'

'Don't be stupid, it's your birthday,' he scoffed. 'This one's on me.'

'No, don't—' He was already gone. She shook her head, fondly exasperated.

The music changed and her face broke into a smile. Closing her eyes, she belted out the lyrics to 'Zombie', bobbing her head to the powerful guitar riffs. She swayed, feeling unaccustomedly sexy in the clingy black dress Paddy had gifted her. It was too short at the back and made her self-conscious every time she bent over, but she knew she looked good in it. This was turning out far better than she had hoped.

Suddenly, she felt hands touching her back and her eyes flew open. Her first thought was that it was Sameer, and she was about to yell at him for startling her. But the words froze in her throat when she found herself looking into the face of a stranger. He was a bit taller than her, had dark curly hair and a glazed look in his eyes. He was expensively dressed in a red Polo T-shirt and black jeans. Aastha thought he would have been quite attractive if not for the fact that he was reeking of alcohol. She turned away, wrinkling her nose in distaste. He had probably thought she was someone else.

She was about to start singing again, when she felt his hands on her arms. 'What the hell?' She tried to pull away.

But instead, his grip tightened to the point of pain and he pulled her back against his body, his sticky breath on the back of her neck. She struggled to get away from him, still half convinced that it was a mistake. His grip was unyielding. Panic set in when she felt his erection pressing against the small of her back and, for a second, she couldn't believe this was happening to her. She fought harder, trying to scream for help. The words came out strangled by fear, and the music was so loud that she couldn't even hear herself.

He let go of one of her arms to wrap an arm securely around her chest, pulling her so close to him she could feel his rancid breath on her ear. He ran his other hand up her dress, squeezing her ass roughly before tugging at the waistband of her underwear. She could feel his fingers at her entrance, pushing in painfully; his breath was sickeningly hot against her ear. She tried to scream again, but no one around them even glanced in her direction. Operating on instinct, she brought her high-heeled shoe down on his foot. He grunted in pain, his grip loosening for just an instant, but it was enough.

She pulled away from him, sobbing, and pushed herself in the direction of the bar. The crowd hindered her movement and she could feel him close behind her. His hands caught the back of her dress once, and she felt it rip as she pulled away. She shoved aside the person in front of her, trying to get as many people between them as possible. Blinded by tears and the flickering strobe lights, she could barely see a thing. Every person who brushed against her sent tremors of fear and revulsion through her body, but she kept moving.

Suddenly, she smashed straight into a man's chest and let out a small scream before her eyes fastened on the familiar message on his T-shirt: 'Do Epic Shit'. She looked up and went limp with relief as she saw Sameer's concerned face looking down at her. She sagged against him, sobbing wildly into his chest, and she could tell he was trying to ask her something. But she couldn't hear him. All she wanted was to get the hell out of there.

Aastha shot up in bed, breathing hard. The high whine of her alarm clock assaulted her ears and she grabbed it and hit the snooze button. Her heart was pounding. She buried her face in her hands and fought for calm, but the nightmare had been too vivid. She blindly reached for her phone, hitting the first number on speed dial.

After a couple of rings, Sameer's sleepy voice answered. 'Hello?'

'Crap,' she said, filled with remorse. 'I didn't mean to wake you—'

'Don't be stupid, you know you can always call me,' he said, instantly alert. 'Nightmare?'

'Yeah.' She sighed. She could already feel her heartbeat slowing at the sound of his voice and felt ashamed that she still needed him to do this for her after all this time. 'I can't believe I still get them. I mean, it's been two years!'

'You're way better than you used to be,' Sameer pointed out. 'When was the last time you had one?'

'A couple of months ago, maybe more,' she said, realizing that he was right.

There had been a time when she'd dreamt about it every single night, when it had kept her up for weeks and painted rings under her eyes. But that had been months ago and she wondered how that one night could still have so much power over her. Oh, it wasn't like she was emotionally crippled, or kept thinking about it every second of the day. But she still started when someone came up behind her, still flinched when any guy other than Sameer touched her.

'I should be over it by now,' she muttered.

'I'm not,' Sameer said, unexpectedly.

'What?'

'You think I'll ever be able to get that out of my head? God, the look on your face—'

'Shut up,' she interrupted him forcefully, shuddering as a fresh wave of images assaulted her.

'Sorry,' he said contritely. 'My point is, it still affects me, and it didn't even happen to me. You should cut yourself a little slack.'

'Yeah,' she said, subdued. 'I guess you're right.' She was unnerved by the thought that he had been scarred by that night too.

'Of course I'm right,' Sameer said firmly. 'So, what plans for the day?'

'I have a manuscript to edit—a really crappy commercial novel by some med student who has no clue how to use a comma.'

Sameer laughed. 'It's just a job, dude. I can't believe how bothered you and Paddy get about this stuff.'

'Not everyone can be as happy-go lucky as you,' Aastha pointed out. 'Besides, bad grammar is a crime.' Sameer cracked up again and she knew she was wasting her breath—the only person who would ever understand her feelings on this subject was Padmini. 'So how's life?' she asked.

'Oh, you know, same old; nothing exciting,' he drawled. 'We have a new project—market research for a Body Shop moisturizer.'

'Do you get free samples?' she asked eagerly.

He laughed. 'I don't think so, but if I do, I'll give them to you. Are we meeting for Game Night?'

'Should be. I'll ask Paddy. We can have dinner first at Ambience Mall and then you guys can come over to my place.'

'Cool,' he said, yawning. 'Let me know.'

'I can hear you falling asleep,' she said. 'I should let you go.'

'Sure you're okay now?'

'I'm fine, really,' she reassured him. 'Thanks, Sam.'

'Any time. See you later.'

He hung up. Aastha took one look at the clock and jumped out of bed. She was running late.

TWO

Padmini Subramanian blinked blearily at the page before her, then glanced at her watch. She almost groaned when she realized she had a full two hours of work left—she didn't think she had enough stamina to last that long.

Who had decided to publish this crap, anyway? It was nowhere near worthy of Axe Publishers. She wished, not for the first time, that she could have been a commissioning editor, so that she could be the one who selected the manuscripts instead of being stuck editing them.

With a frustrated sigh, she reached for her cell phone. Her mood turned even sourer when she saw that her boyfriend hadn't bothered to text her, even after the fight they'd had the previous night.

I hate boys, she texted Aastha in a fit of annoyance. *And pretentious literary fiction.*

Aastha's reply came ten seconds later. *I know, right?* ☺

Seriously, what the hell does 'The twilight broke like weak, diluted coffee' even mean?

The manuscript I'm editing is worse. Are you fighting with Rahul again?

Then, before Padmini could reply, another text. *Btw, we're meeting for Game Night tonight. My place.*

Padmini made a face; she had completely forgotten about that. *Yeah, it was a pretty bad fight. Not sure we'll be up for it.*

You guys have to come. Why are you fighting, anyway?

Padmini hesitated. She really wasn't in the mood to hear Aastha waxing eloquent about how Rahul wasn't good enough for her. But she was feeling too sorry for herself today and needed to vent. *There's this chick he works with named Natasha. She keeps flirting with him, but he says they're just friends. I dunno. It's just pissing off. Maybe I'm being too possessive.*

Doubt it, came the instant response. *After Purnima, you have every right not to trust him.*

Padmini felt a flare of irritation. Even though Purnima was the reason she was so paranoid, it annoyed her that Aastha kept bringing her up. *You know, he didn't actually do anything with her,* she typed. *And that was ages ago.* Padmini didn't know whom she was trying to convince.

I know, Aastha replied. *Look, go meet him, work things out, and then we can all meet for dinner and head to my place.*

Padmini wavered. She wanted Rahul to be the one to make the first move and call her for once, but she knew it wouldn't happen. *Yeah, okay*, she texted back. *See you later.*

Moodily, she texted Rahul and told him to come to her house after work so they could talk. His reply was a terse '*ok.*' She frowned and then sighed, resigning herself to another tedious argument.

Later that night Aastha sat alone in Kobe Sizzlers, fiddling with her napkin. She had been waiting for her friends for more than twenty minutes now, and her stomach was rumbling with hunger. She pulled out her phone and was just about to call Padmini when Sameer walked in.

'What took you so long?' she asked in an annoyed tone.

'Traffic,' said Sameer. 'You know how bad it can get at peak hour. And why are you grousing at me? It looks like I'm not the only one running late.' He raised an eyebrow significantly at the two empty seats.

'I know, but I'm seriously starving to death,' Aastha said. 'Let's order a starter.'

Fifteen minutes later, they had finished most of the garlic bread and there was still no sign of Padmini or Rahul. Neither of them was responding to phone calls either. 'Where are they?' Sameer frowned. 'This is irritating.'

'They've been fighting again.' Aastha shook her head. 'Rahul can be such a douchebag sometimes. I don't know why she took him back after Purnima. I mean, I know he didn't technically cheat, but still.'

'Purnima was her hostel friend, right?' Sameer asked. He had been working during Aastha and Paddy's postgrad years, and had missed a lot of gossip because of his distance from Delhi University's famed North Campus.

'Yeah, she was madly in love with him. She'd keep texting him and then there was Elizabeth's birthday party . . . he danced with her for an hour.'

'Oh yeah.' Sameer shot her a bemused look. 'How do you keep track of this stuff? You weren't even *at* the party.'

Aastha snorted. 'Please, like I could forget after Paddy called me at two in the morning crying her eyes out. By the way, how's Karuna?'

Karuna was Sameer's girlfriend. She had shifted to Bangalore after her postgraduation. Sameer sighed. 'She's fine, but her parents are being damn annoying,' he said angrily.

'Why, what happened?'

'They want her to get married now. Seems there's some guy they want her to meet, some Joseph Thomas. He's apparently the ultimate catch—IIT and IIMA!'

'Really? What are you guys going to do?' Aastha asked.

Sameer shrugged. 'Wait for it to blow over, I guess. I mean, it's not like she'll say yes to him.'

'You don't think it might be more serious than that?' Aastha said cautiously. 'She's twenty-three now, isn't she? Orthodox parents start freaking out about marriage and stuff at that age. I have a whole heap of relatives like that in my extended family and they've already started hinting to my parents.' Thankfully, her own parents were more broad-minded and had no intention of marrying her off any time soon.

'They can't possibly expect her to say yes to the first guy they throw her way,' Sameer said dismissively. 'She just has to be firm, that's all.'

Aastha's misgivings were not diminished by Sameer's casual words. Because his own parents were very liberal, he was sometimes ridiculously oblivious to how the rest of the world worked. She was about to question him further about Karuna when Paddy and Rahul walked in.

'You guys are early,' Sameer said sarcastically.

'Sorry, traffic,' Padmini said as she sat down.

'The hickey on your neck tells a different tale,' Aastha sang, and Padmini blushed and laughed.

'Shall we order?' Rahul cut in, looking uncomfortable.

'Yes, please, I'm starving,' Sameer said.

They ordered their sizzlers and then Sameer said, 'So, I was thinking we could play Risk tonight.'

Aastha brightened. She knew it was a bit unusual for people her age to meet once a week to play board games, but she looked forward to it all week. And Risk was one of her favourite games: it was competitive and did not take too much mental effort.

But Paddy groaned. 'Risk takes way too long. Can't we play Taboo or something?'

'It's Friday and you're twenty-four!' Sameer exclaimed, 'Don't tell me you've already lost the ability to pull an all-nighter.'

'I'm tired of Game Night,' Rahul said unexpectedly. 'Can't we do something else for once? Go to a club, like normal people do?'

Aastha's breath caught, but before she could say anything, Sameer cut in sharply, 'You know we can't do that.'

Rahul sighed. 'Oh, right, I forgot. Sorry.'

Aastha stared down at her plate, suddenly feeling very small. She had never been able to set foot in a club after that night, but it had never occurred to her that she might be holding the others back. 'You guys can go if you want to,' she said. 'Seriously, I'll be okay at ho—'

'No,' Sameer said forcefully. 'We're having Game Night, just like always.'

After a short tense silence, Padmini changed the subject. 'So, we need to book a hotel for the Goa trip.' Everyone brightened.

They had all been looking forward to the trip for ages and now it was only a month away.

'What budget are we looking at?' Rahul asked.

'The max I can afford is a thousand bucks a night,' Aastha said. 'Actually, less would be better.'

'It should be decent, though,' said Sameer, who had always loved his material comforts.

As they discussed their plans, Aastha's mind drifted back to Rahul's words. Most young working people enjoyed going clubbing. Her flatmate, Nainika, went every other weekend. Had she been holding her friends back? Could she not give it a try, just this once? She shuddered at the thought. Not yet. But then she didn't want the others to suffer. She resolved to talk to Sameer about it as soon as she got the chance.

THREE

Sameer shifted restlessly on Aastha's bed. Risk had been amazing fun. He and Aastha had made an alliance and taken over Europe and Asia between them. By the time the game got over, it was past 3 a.m., so Sameer had decided to sleep over. Unfortunately, Aastha's mattress was very uncomfortable.

'Sam,' Aastha sighed from beside him as he shifted again. 'Could you stop moving around? I'm trying to sleep, here.'

'How the hell do you sleep on this every night?' Sameer asked, irritated. 'This mattress is as hard as nails.'

'You are such a spoilt brat, Sameer Mascarenas,' she drawled sleepily. 'One would think you've been living your entire life in luxury hotels.'

'This is so not a luxury thing,' he protested. 'Paddy says the same whenever she sleeps here. Only *you* would be able to sleep on something this hard and not wind up with bruises.'

She snorted, amused. 'Just turn over and lie on your stomach, princess. That way it won't dig into your bones.'

He did as she said and found the position only somewhat more bearable. 'You're insane not to replace this piece of crap,' he grumbled. 'I still don't understand why you had to give

Rahul and Paddy Nainika's room.' Nainika was away that night and her bed was a lot more comfortable.

'They just made up after a bad fight,' Aastha reminded him, pulling her blanket more securely around herself.

'They're *always* fighting and making up,' Sameer said grumpily. 'And they live, like, five minutes away from each other.'

'I know, but still . . .'

They were silent for a few minutes. Then just as Sameer was falling asleep, Aastha's soft voice floated across the darkness. 'Hey, can I ask you something?'

'Hmmm.'

'Do you—I mean, if you ever wanted to go clubbing, you'd go, right? You guys wouldn't hold back for my sake?'

All traces of sleep gone, Sameer sat up in bed. He could have killed Rahul for bringing this up. 'Aastha, believe me when I say that going clubbing is the *last* thing on anyone's priority list. Rahul was just being—'

'Paddy might want to go,' Aastha interrupted. 'She didn't say no when he brought it up. I just don't want to hold you guys back from having fun because of my issues.'

'Are you serious, Aastha?' Sameer asked, incredulously. 'Paddy didn't say anything because she'd just made up with him and didn't want to get into a fight again. Do you really think she would ever want to step into a pub after that night? It could have just as easily been her.'

He felt Aastha tremble beside him. 'Don't say that,' she said sharply.

'Sorry.' He felt guilty for having upset her. 'My point is, stop feeling so bad about this. If we want to dance and drink and listen to loud music, we can just as easily do that here. You have speakers.'

'Yeah,' she said in a lighter tone. 'I guess you're right.'

'Of course I'm right,' Sameer said. 'Now get some sleep, will you?' He smiled at her and lay down.

'Sure. Goodnight, Sam.'

Soon she was sound asleep.

Sameer lay awake for a long time, listening to the rhythmic sound of her breathing. He remembered that night again. He could still feel Aastha sobbing into his chest, refusing to answer any of his questions about what had happened. He'd practically had to carry her outside because she had been trembling so violently. Neither Padmini nor Rahul had answered his calls, so he had left them behind and driven her back to his flat.

It was only when she'd stumbled out of the car that he'd seen that her dress was torn at the back and realized what had happened. He had never been so furious in his life. If he hadn't had to take care of her, he would have gone back to the club and tried to find the guy who had done this so he could beat the shit out of him. He'd cursed himself for leaving her alone to get the drinks.

He had helped her up to his apartment. In the light of his living room, he had seen marks on her arms in the shape of fingers and had felt suddenly cold as he wondered how far the assault had gone.

The first thing she had wanted to do was to take a shower and she had spent so long in the bathroom that he'd been afraid she had passed out. She had emerged dressed in the T-shirt and track pants he had given her, her eyes bloodshot and devastated. In that moment, all traces of her strong-willed vibrant personality had disappeared.

She had spent the night on the sofa, curled up in his arms. She had refused to let go of him even when Paddy and Rahul had arrived hours later. Padmini had hovered in the background for a few moments, and then she had sat cross-legged in front of the sofa and tried to take Aastha's hand. But Aastha had pulled away with an inarticulate cry.

Sameer had known, in that moment, that it would be up to him to get her through this, and he had vowed that he wouldn't let her down. Aastha had leaned on him without hesitation in the months that followed.

Over the past year, he had watched her strong personality reassert itself slowly and he had been so proud of her. He was angry with Rahul for even considering the idea of going clubbing again. Grimly, he resolved to have a word with him the next morning to make sure he didn't bring it up again. Slowly, he drifted into sleep.

'I'm telling you, you're overreacting. I'm sure it'll just blow over if you keep telling them no.'

Aastha opened her eyes. Sameer was sitting on the edge of the bed, his back tense. She realized he was probably talking to Karuna.

'So go ahead and agree to meet him, and then say you didn't like him! No one can *force* you to get married to him—'

Aastha cringed at the sound of Karuna's shrill angry voice interrupting him.

'I know that, but what do you expect *me* to do about it?' Sameer said. 'Hello? Damn it, you did not just hang up on me!'

'You are such an idiot,' Aastha said, sitting up and leaning back against the headboard.

He turned around to face her, annoyed. 'Really? Then please explain how exactly this is *my* fault.'

'First of all, you shouldn't have told her that she's overreacting when her parents are pressuring her into marriage! Don't you realize that this is her worst nightmare?'

He scoffed. 'Please, it's not like they can actually *make* her—'

'Maybe not,' she interrupted. 'But they can definitely make her life miserable if they want to. She's probably going through hell and you just made it ten times worse by acting like a complete douche.'

He frowned angrily and grumbled, 'How the hell is this any of your business, anyway?'

She ignored him. 'If you have any sense, you'll call her back and apologize before it gets worse.'

'No,' he said stonily. 'This is not my fault.' He rose and strode towards the bathroom, slamming the door shut.

Aastha flopped back into bed with a frustrated sigh. Sometimes Sameer could be the most stubborn and pig-headed idiot she knew.

She tried to go back to sleep, but found herself unable to now that she had woken up. She rose and made the bed, and then joined Sameer in the living room, where he was sitting on the sofa, sipping a cup of coffee.

He cast an apologetic look in her direction. 'Sorry if I woke you.'

She waved this away dismissively and went to the kitchen to get her own mug.

Soon Rahul and Padmini joined them, and they spent the rest of the morning lazing around.

Just before they left, Rahul drew Aastha aside and apologized for his behaviour the previous night. 'I shouldn't have said that,' he said rather gruffly. 'It was insensitive and I'm really sorry.'

'That's okay,' Aastha said awkwardly. 'Just forget about it.'

She wondered if Padmini had said something to him, then decided it didn't really matter. It was one of the things she appreciated about Rahul—he always owned up to his mistakes.

She spent the rest of the day proofreading a manuscript that was due first thing on Monday.

Sometimes she truly envied Sameer. He didn't particularly enjoy his job, but it paid him handsomely and that had always been the thing he cared about most. She wished that her priorities could have been that simple. She would probably have felt a lot better about her own job if it had paid her more than peanuts.

The problem was that a master's in English didn't leave her with many options. She didn't want to go abroad and study further like some of her classmates were doing, nor did she find the thought of teaching appealing. So she would have to continue working in publishing. She looked at the pile of sheets on her lap. She had eighty more pages left to proofread. With a sigh, she tried to focus on her work.

———

The following week passed fairly uneventfully, until Aastha received a phone call from Padmini on Thursday afternoon. 'Hey, what's up?' she asked, surprised that her friend was calling her at work.

'I'm freaking out,' Padmini said shakily.

'What happened?'

'I . . . I just keep fighting with Rahul. And he won't stop talking to that bitch. She's all over his fucking Facebook page. He keeps saying there's nothing going on, but I don't think he's even told her he has a girlfriend!'

'Are you serious?' Aastha exclaimed loudly, outraged. Several of her colleagues glanced up, and she lowered her voice. 'How can you let him get away with that?'

'And what am I supposed to do about it, exactly?' Padmini asked.

'I don't know, say you won't talk to him till he tells her, or—'

'That's not even what I'm most upset about,' she interrupted. 'I keep throwing up. It only started a couple of days ago . . . I guess I could just be sick, but—' She hesitated. 'I'm also late . . .'

Holy crap. 'Just give me a second, okay?' Aastha said, not wanting to talk about this in public. She rose and headed for a more secluded spot. 'How late?'

'Five days,' Padmini said. 'That never happens.'

'But you guys always use condoms, right?' Aastha asked.

'Yeah, but you know how they break sometimes . . .' Paddy replied. 'Aastha, I don't know what to do. This is scaring the shit out of me,' she said nervously.

'Hang on. First of all, have you told Rahul about this?' Aastha asked.

'I can't,' Padmini said. 'He'll freak out. Besides, I don't even know for sure that I *am*.'

'Then that's the first thing we need to find out,' said Aastha, trying to sound reassuring. 'I'll come over to your place today after work. I'll buy a pregnancy test kit from a chemist and then we can find out for sure.'

'Yeah,' Padmini said in a stilted voice, 'okay.'

'Look, you most probably aren't pregnant,' Aastha tried to reassure her. 'And if you are, it's not like it's the end of the world. There are lots of options. One of Nainika's friends went through this last year and she got it taken care of without too much trouble. We'll figure it out.'

'Yeah,' Padmini said, sounding a bit calmer. 'Thanks, Aastha.'

'Any time. Don't drive yourself too crazy, okay? I'll see you later.'

FOUR

One of the best things about Aastha was how decisive she was, Padmini reflected as she paced the length of her apartment. She had been toying with the idea of buying a pregnancy test kit for three days now, but had been too cowardly to do it. And Aastha, as soon as she had found out, had immediately jumped into action. That was why she had called her rather than Karuna.

Well, no, she conceded. She would have called Karuna too, if her friend had not been going through World War III at home. Padmini and Karuna had been close friends since primary school. They had come to Delhi University together and, though they'd gone to different colleges, they had kept in touch. In fact, it was through Padmini that Karuna and Sameer had met in the first place. She had been so excited—Sameer was such a wonderful guy and the two had seemed so perfect for each other. For five years they had seemed to Paddy like the ideal couple. She hoped their relationship would survive this storm.

Her thoughts were interrupted by the sound of the doorbell. 'Hey,' said Aastha, making a beeline for the single sofa in the living room and flopping down on it. 'You'll never believe this. My landlady walked into the shop just as the chemist was

handing me the kit! She looked so horrified. I'll never be able
to look her in the eye again.'

'So you got it, then?' Padmini asked. Her heart was
pounding and she was feeling nauseous again.

'Here.' Aastha rummaged in her bag for a moment and
handed her a small packet.

'Fuck!' Padmini said nervously, clutching it in her hands.
'I can't do this.' If she was pregnant, she honestly didn't know
what she would do.

'Yes, you can!' Aastha said. When Padmini continued to
hesitate, she added, 'Isn't it worse not to know for sure? Now
get into the bathroom right now and don't come out until
you've peed on that thing.'

Trembling, Padmini entered the bathroom, emerging two
minutes later.

'Well?' Aastha demanded.

'Don't know yet.' Padmini was shifting her weight from
foot to foot. 'It takes a couple of minutes.'

They waited outside the bathroom door, tense and silent.
After a few minutes, Aastha asked, 'Isn't it time?'

Padmini stared at the door, full of trepidation. She couldn't
bring herself to go inside. Aastha glanced at her, read her
indecision and strode into the bathroom herself.

'Aastha, don't—I just peed on that thing—'

'It's negative!' Aastha called out.

'What?'

'It's negative, you're not pregnant!' She emerged, beaming.

Padmini's knees had gone weak with relief. 'Thank God!'
she whispered, stumbling over to the sofa and sitting down. 'I
am never having sex again,' she declared with feeling.

Aastha burst out laughing. 'Yeah, right. I am so going to quote you the next time you and Rahul want to sneak off into some corner like horny teenagers.'

'We're not that bad,' Padmini protested half-heartedly.

'Yes, you are,' Aastha said. 'But I don't really care about that right now; we have to celebrate! Shall we order pizza?'

Padmini nodded, her stomach growling suddenly at the mention of food. Since morning, she had been too keyed up to eat anything. 'And Giani's ice cream,' she said. 'My treat.'

'You don't have to——'

'Yeah, I do,' Padmini said. If it hadn't been for Aastha, she would still have been going out of her mind with worry. 'You're staying over, right? We can watch an old chick flick. *Devil Wears Prada* or *Legally Blonde,* you choose.' They were the most fluffy, feel-good movies she could think of.

'*Devil Wears Prada*,' said Aastha.

Padmini smiled. 'Sounds great,' she said.

————

Rahul Mitra was completely exhausted. Work had been crazy lately. But instead of going straight home, as he so badly wanted to, he was driving to Padmini's house in Malviya Nagar, which, thankfully, was only five minutes away from his own. They had been fighting too much lately and he was tired of it. It was time to smooth things over.

Not that there was any justification for her possessive behaviour. Natasha was just a good friend who happened to be very active on Facebook. Padmini had always been paranoid after his flirtation with Purnima, but that had been ages ago!

Didn't she know that Rahul would never do anything like that again?

It was Aastha who always kept bringing it up, who never let her forget it. Rahul was sick of her judgemental attitude. What right did she have to interfere in his relationship? He wished Paddy would stop confiding in her so much.

Using his spare key, he let himself into the apartment. The living room was dark and silent, and Padmini's bedroom door was closed. She was asleep, then. He pictured tiptoeing in and kissing her awake, but headed for the bathroom first. He flicked on the light. His eyes fell on what looked like a thermometer lying by the sink.

Was Padmini sick?

He looked more closely, frowning in confusion as he realized it wasn't a thermometer at all. And then his eyes fell on an empty box lying on the ground. Prega News. *What the fuck?* Heart pounding, he stared closely at what could only be a pregnancy test—but it was no longer showing any result. Was Paddy . . . ?

He turned and strode into her bedroom, flicking on the tube light. He stopped short when he saw that she wasn't alone. Why had Padmini called Aastha and not him? Angry and alarmed, he shook his girlfriend awake.

'Wha—Rahul? What are you—?'

'Outside,' he hissed, grabbing her arm and pulling her into the living room. He slammed the bedroom door shut and faced her, breathing hard. 'Are you pregnant?'

A look of dismayed realization swept over her face. 'No, I—it was negative.'

Relief swept over him and he closed his eyes. *Thank God!*

'I'm sorry I scared you,' Paddy continued. 'I forgot to throw it away, Aastha was—'

His anger returned in full force. 'You thought you were pregnant and the first thing you did was call Aastha?!' he shouted. 'I'm your boyfriend! Don't you think I deserved—'

'And when, exactly, was I supposed to call you?' she fired back, 'While you were flirting with Natasha? Spending late nights at the office—'

'Are you fucking serious?' Rahul asked incredulously. 'How many times do I have to tell you that nothing is going on between me and Natasha? She is just a friend!'

'A friend who doesn't even know I exist—'

Rahul slammed his hand against a wall. For a moment, they stared at each other in shock, both startled by the force of his anger. Then Rahul said through gritted teeth, 'You do not get to use Natasha as an excuse for not telling me about this!'

'I would have told you if there was anything to tell!' Padmini exclaimed. 'What was the point of freaking you out for no reason?'

'Let me get this straight,' Rahul said. 'If I hadn't come to your house today and seen that test next to the sink, I would never have found out about any of this?'

'That's not what I—'

'Yeah, it was. Just—fuck you. I can't even look at you right now.'

Seething, he strode out of the house, slamming the front door behind him.

FIVE

Aastha winced as she heard the screech of tyres that signalled Rahul pulling away from the house. She waited, wondering what she should do. Paddy was probably beside herself and ordinarily, Aastha would not have hesitated to check on her. But she had overheard enough of the argument to know that she had been one of the reasons for the fight and she wondered if Paddy would be very happy to see her right then.

After a few minutes of indecision, she got out of bed. Paddy wasn't in the living room, but the bathroom light was on.

'Hey, you okay?' she called through the door.

'Sick.'

Aastha flinched at the sound of retching. *No wonder she'd thought she was pregnant.*

Paddy emerged a couple of minutes later, looking completely drained and exhausted.

'You really are ill,' Aastha said. 'How long has this been going on?'

'A couple of days.' Padmini flopped down on the sofa. 'I'm assuming you heard most of that fight?'

'Yeah.' She sat down beside her friend and slung an arm around her shoulders.

'I can't believe I forgot to throw the test away,' Padmini said. 'Fucking careless.'

'It's okay,' she said. 'He'll forgive you. You guys always work things out eventually.'

'And then we always end up fighting again,' Paddy said, tiredly. 'What's the point?'

'Most relationships are like that, though,' Aastha pointed out.

'Not all the time. Sometimes I think we should just end it, you know? It's so exhausting.'

'I'm sure it'll all work out,' she told her friend. 'Say you're sorry; tell him you freaked out and didn't handle it very well. I'm sure he can understand that.'

'I hope so.' She sighed. 'Let's just go back to sleep.'

The next morning, Padmini was listless and obviously still unwell. She picked unenthusiastically at her breakfast. Rahul was refusing to return her calls and, even though Aastha had told her to give him some space, she couldn't seem to leave it alone. Thankfully, she didn't have much time to brood, since they both had to leave for work.

It was a Friday and, by some rare miracle, Aastha didn't have any work to do over the weekend. She wanted to take advantage of the rare free time by spending the weekend with her friends, but unfortunately, Game Night wasn't a possibility until Rahul and Paddy had made up with each other.

Perhaps she could meet up with Sameer. It was rare for them not to see each other two or three times a week since they both lived in Gurgaon. She texted him, asking if he was free to meet for lunch the next day.

cant, came the reply, *going to Blore 4 the weeknd.*

Oh, say hi to Karuna for me! Very romantic of you to surprise her like this. ☺

actually, its 4 work, Sameer texted back. *they were gonna send me next week 4 the Body Shop project. i asked the HR people if i cud go earlier.*

Nice. When are you back?

Tue evening.

Okay, have a good trip!

Aastha couldn't quite repress the sigh of disappointment as she set down her phone. Although she was glad Sameer was getting to meet Karuna, she hated having nothing to do over the weekend. She consoled herself with the thought that Nainika would be home, and that meant her friends would come over to drink and smoke up. Though she didn't have a lot in common with them, they were warm and friendly people, and always fun to hang out with.

———

It was half past two and everyone but Nainika's boyfriend, Avinash, had left an hour ago. Aastha knew she should sleep, but she wasn't feeling tired. She sat on the floor leaning against the sofa, her laptop perched on her knees as she checked her Facebook notifications.

On the beanbag next to her, Avinash exhaled a puff of hookah smoke in her direction. 'Dude, could you not do that in my face!' she exclaimed, shifting away from him.

'Sorry!' said Avinash. He took another drag and handed the hose to Nainika, who was curled up beside him.

'One would think you'd be used to it by now,' her flatmate said with a laugh. 'I still can't believe you haven't tried it even once.'

Aastha snorted. 'You sound like that friend of yours, Kabir,' she said. Kabir had spent half the evening flirting with her and the other half persuading her to smoke, claiming she didn't know what she was missing. 'Where did you find him, anyway?'

'He's new at the office,' Nainika said. 'He's really cute, right?'

'I'm sitting right here,' Avinash protested mildly and she placated him with a kiss on the cheek.

'He was okay,' Aastha said with a shrug. She had been too annoyed by his hovering to really notice.

'He seemed to think you were pretty *okay*, too,' Nainika said, wiggling her eyebrows suggestively. 'Want me to set you guys up?'

'No, thank you,' Aastha said, grimacing. Nainika was always trying to set her up with somebody or the other.

'But *why not*?' Nainika asked. 'You know, I don't get you. You're good-looking, you're smart, you've got everything going for you, but every time a guy even tries to get to know you, you're just not interested! Do you just not want to date anyone? Ever?'

'I—it's not that I'm not interested,' Aastha said, a little taken aback. 'It's just . . .'

She trailed off, not knowing what to say. The truth was, she did get lonely. She didn't like to think about it too often, but it wasn't easy being the only single person in her friends' circle. That sense of closeness between Paddy and Rahul, the way Nainika was so comfortable lying next to Avinash—she wanted that too. But how was she supposed to even think of dating anyone when she still jumped out of her skin every time a guy touched her?

'I just can't,' she said.

'Why not?'

Aastha hesitated. She had met Nainika almost a year ago, through a classmate who had put them in touch because they both needed someone to stay with. After living with her for so many months, Aastha considered her a close friend. But she didn't know about the incident in F-Bar, and she knew Nainika would keep pushing until she told her the truth. The problem was that Aastha had never actually had to talk about what had happened. All her friends had already known.

'Okay, you know how I don't go clubbing?' she asked.

'Yeah . . . ?' Nainika frowned, confused by the abrupt change of subject.

'There's a reason for that,' Aastha continued. 'A couple of years ago, I went to F-Bar for my birthday. And this guy kind of . . . he—uh, got too close. It wasn't, you know, as bad as it could have been but—' Fuck, she wasn't making any sense at all! 'Anyway. After that, I don't go to clubs or bars, and I don't like it when people, especially guys, get too close to me. That's why I don't date.'

'Is that why you get startled whenever I touch you?' Avinash asked, looking stricken. 'I never meant to make you uncomfortable—'

'It's not you,' Aastha said hurriedly, meeting his concerned gaze. 'It's everyone. It's just a physical reaction. I'll get over it eventually.'

Neither Nainika nor Avinash looked reassured by this and Aastha didn't blame them. After all, it had been two years since that night, and she could tell they were drawing conclusions about how bad the assault had to have been for her to still be this affected. But they hadn't seen her then; they had no idea of the progress she had made. There had been a time when she couldn't even bear Padmini touching her, but now she didn't even notice when she did.

'You don't jump when Sameer touches you,' said Nainika suddenly. 'I've seen him put his arm around you a few times and you don't act uncomfortable.'

Aastha shrugged. 'He was there that night,' she said. 'He took care of me after it happened and he was a really good friend to me. I guess I just feel safe around him.'

'Do you have a thing for him?' Avinash asked. 'I've always wondered. You just seem so close.'

'He has a girlfriend,' said Aastha quickly.

'Doesn't mean you can't still have a thing for him,' Nainika said.

'No way,' said Aastha. 'He's just a really good friend.'

Nainika didn't look convinced. Aastha could sense she wanted to probe further, but she was in no mood to discuss it. She muttered something about feeling sleepy and went to her room.

SIX

Karuna Mary Thomas hurried into Koshy's, cursing the Bangalore traffic for having delayed her. Her anger melted and her face broke into a smile when she caught sight of Sameer. He was sitting at a corner table studying the menu; he hadn't seen her yet.

She wanted to rush up to him, but checked herself, scanning the restaurant for anyone who might recognize her. It was unlikely that she would run into a family member on this side of the city, but it didn't hurt to be careful. Sameer spotted her when she was halfway across the room and stood up, opening his arms invitingly. She crashed into his arms and he hugged her tightly.

'It is so good to see you,' he said into her hair. 'It's been way too long.'

'I know,' she said, hugging him back just as hard.

After years of meeting every day in North Campus, long distance had not been an easy adjustment. Karuna had badly wanted to stay and work in Delhi after her postgraduation, but her parents had insisted that she come back home. Since she had just started writing the actuaries, a set of exams which, when she passed them all, would make her a certified analyst and significantly increase her earning potential, she had decided to humour them. She spent most of her time attending coaching classes and studying for her exams. Sameer spoke to her on the phone every day, and he made it a point to come down to Bangalore once every few months, but it hadn't been the same.

Reluctantly, they pulled away and sat down. 'So how long do I have with you?' he asked. 'Can you come back to my hotel after coffee?'

'I wish,' said Karuna. 'I've only got two hours; my parents think I'm in coaching.'

Sameer groaned.

Karuna let him suffer for a few seconds and then added with a grin, 'But I can give you tomorrow night. I told my parents I'm going over to a friend's to study.'

Sameer looked as though Christmas had come early. 'I am so totally in love with you,' he declared, grabbing her hand under the table.

She laughed, feeling a rush of affection for him. They ordered their food, chatting about random things. Karuna couldn't keep the smile off her face. She hadn't realized how much she had missed Sameer till he was right in front of her. She decided, then and there, that she wouldn't dampen the mood today by mentioning her parents.

'How's Paddy?' she asked. 'I haven't heard from her in a few days.'

'She's okay,' Sameer said. 'I think she's been fighting with Rahul a lot lately, which is hardly new.'

'Oh, that sucks.' She wondered why Paddy hadn't mentioned it. 'What about Aastha, how is she?'

'Same as always,' Sameer said fondly. 'She's doing a lot better now.'

'Glad to hear it,' said Karuna, and she was. She had only met Aastha a few times, but had heard a lot about her from Sameer and Padmini. They had drawn a picture of a girl who was kind-hearted and fiercely loyal to her friends, though a little self-righteous and not very good at minding her own business. Sameer had spent a great deal of time with her after she'd been assaulted, but Karuna had never grudged him that. It could just as easily have happened to her.

They continued to chat as they ate. Karuna was having such a good time that she stayed for longer than she had planned and ended the reaching home late.

'Where were you?' her mother demanded as soon as she walked into the house.

'There was a lot of traffic,' she said, hoping she wouldn't be asked any more questions. But when her mother pursed her lips in disapproval, Karuna felt that familiar surge of suffocation. Things had been so tense lately, and not just because of their constant arguments. Ever since she had told them she didn't want to get married, they had been watching her like hawks. Karuna wondered what they were so afraid of. They didn't know she had a boyfriend.

'Your father and I want to talk to you after dinner,' her mother said, 'about Joseph.'

Karuna groaned aloud. 'Amma, not again—'

'Yes, again,' she said firmly. 'It's important.'

Great! Karuna thought angrily as she headed to her room. *Another round of How to Get Karuna to Marry the Super Eligible IIT–IIM Guy. It was going to be so much fun.*

And when they all sat down together, Karuna was expecting her parents to start off as they usually did—by telling her what a nice boy Joseph Thomas was, how respectable and qualified his family was, and how they only wanted what was best for her. Then they would plead with her to meet him just once, for their sakes, and then she'd say no, and they'd keep arguing about it until Karuna lost her patience and stormed out. She'd already been through too many variations of the conversation to be apprehensive.

So she was surprised and a little alarmed when her parents sat her down in the living room with unusually grim, determined expressions on their faces. Something was different this time.

Her father was never one to beat about the bush and he didn't waste any time in getting to the point. 'Karuna, we are getting tired of your attitude,' he said. 'You are not a child any more.'

'I know that, Appa,' Karuna blurted out. 'So could you please stop treating me like one?'

Her father's expression darkened. 'Acting smart is not going to help you,' he warned her. 'We've just been told that Joseph is going to America for the next two months on work—apparently, it was at very short notice. There's no need to look so happy about it,' he added sharply. 'His family is very disappointed that you two haven't even talked yet. We told them that you would be calling him tomorrow.'

Karuna's jaw set. 'I am *not* going to—' she began.

'Yes, you are,' he said firmly. 'If you don't, we'll cut off your pocket money and you won't step out of the house except to go for coaching.'

Karuna stared at him in disbelief. 'Are you serious?' she croaked. 'I am twenty-three years old! You can't just ground me!'

'Yes, we can,' her father said grimly. 'I will not have you ruining your life because of some childish impulse to be independent. It's not easy to find good matches these days. Do you want to end up like your cousin? Thirty years old and they still haven't found anyone for her. And why? Because her parents started looking too late. I am not making that mistake.'

'And Joseph went to your school,' her mother interjected. 'He's from your generation, your mindset. If you—'

'I don't want to marry him, Amma,' Karuna said, her eyes filling with tears. 'Or anyone else, for that matter. Can't you understand that?'

'No, I can't.' Her mother sounded genuinely bewildered. 'You haven't even met him yet!'

Her father stood up. 'Don't force us to make your life more difficult than it has to be, sweetheart,' he said softly. 'You'll thank us for this later.'

Unable to stand it any more, she walked out of the room in numb disbelief. She had never thought they would go this far, not in a million years. Threatening to take away her freedom to go out, to visit friends—the only things that made her life in Bangalore bearable. It made her stomach clench just to think of it. Could she bear to stay at home all the time, fighting her parents every second of the day? She would go insane.

In that moment, she truly hated her parents. She was financially dependent on them because she wasn't working and here they were using it against her. She had a feeling that it wouldn't be the last time they did.

As she dialled Joseph's number the next afternoon, Karuna told herself that this didn't have to be that big a deal if she didn't want it to be. She knew it was just a conversation and, thankfully, Joseph would be out of the country for the next couple of months, which would buy her some time. But it still felt a little like she was cheating on Sameer and she was sure he would react badly when she told him.

'Hello,' said a deep male voice on the other end.

'Hi,' she said nervously. 'This is Karuna Mary Thomas.'

There was a pause, then he said, 'Oh, hi! My parents said you might be calling.'

'Yeah,' she said awkwardly.

When she didn't add anything, he said, 'So, apparently you went to St Mary's too? Which batch?'

'2007,' she said.

'Oh, really?' he said. 'I'm three batches senior to you.'

'I don't remember you in high school,' she said.

He snorted. 'Yes, you do. Remember Tanya Kapur? She used to lead the choir.'

'Tanya Kapur—wait, you're *that* Joseph? The Joseph-and-Tanya Joseph?'

'Guilty as charged.'

Joseph and Tanya had been famous in school—they had started dating in the eighth standard, which at the time was still rare enough to horrify their teachers. Most of the students had thought the pairing very romantic—they were both good-looking, Tanya was a brilliant student and Joseph had been in the cricket team, so they had seemed like the perfect couple. They had stayed together till they graduated from high school and probably would have continued dating if

Tanya had not gone abroad for college.

For some reason, the realization that he'd been in a relationship in high school shocked Karuna. She had imagined a very stereotypical, geeky guy who was nothing more than his qualifications, but she realized her mother had been right—he really was from her generation.

'You know, we used to gossip about you all the time,' she said. 'Which was probably not as much fun for you as it was for us.'

'You can say that again,' he said wryly. 'With that many people talking, our parents always found out whenever we went out anywhere. It was a nightmare.'

She could picture it so clearly—the fights with the parents, the lies they both must have told, the way they must have had to sneak around and ask their friends to cover for them. If Sameer had been in Bangalore, she would probably have had to do the same. In that moment of empathy, she wanted nothing more than to tell him the truth about Sameer. She was sure he would understand.

But she couldn't take the risk. Not yet. The Malayali Christian community in Bangalore was very tightly knit and, if Joseph said something in front of the wrong person, her parents would find out and all hell would break loose.

She asked him something about one of his classmates and they spent the next fifteen minutes reminiscing about school. When she hung up, she wasn't feeling nearly as miserable about the conversation as she had thought she would, which made her feel even more guilty.

She was not looking forward to Sameer's reaction when she told him about this phone call that night.

Surprisingly, Sameer's reaction wasn't what Karuna had expected. She told him everything about her conversation with Joseph and his only response was, 'So this is good, right?'

Karuna blinked, not sure she'd heard him correctly. She shifted on the bed and asked, 'What?'

'You spoke to him, so your parents will lay off you for a while,' Sameer said. 'And he's off to the US for two months, which means the whole thing has been delayed for the time being.'

He tried to pull her closer, but she resisted. 'Are you seriously this oblivious?' she asked incredulously. 'Don't you care that I kept swearing I'd never talk to him and now I have? You should see how happy my parents are. They think if I agreed to this, I'll agree the next time they tell me to call him, and then, when they ask me to meet him, and when they—'

He interrupted her with a long-suffering sigh which made her blood boil. 'Karuna, you really are overreacting, you know? You need to remember something—they can't *force you* to marry him. Just say no if it comes to that.'

It wasn't the first time he had told her this and it always made her blood boil when he did. 'I can't just say no,' she said heatedly. 'They can make my life completely miserable if they want to. You have no idea. You need to get it through your head just how serious they are.'

'Fine,' he said, rolling his eyes. 'It's very serious. What am I supposed to do about it? We can't do anything till it actually happens, so can you just chill? I don't want us to fight when I'm only here for two days.'

Karuna's eyes stung. She knew he was only being logical; that she had a tendency to worry too much. He had often said similar things to her during college when she was anxious about her exam results and it had helped then. But this was their future at stake and he was treating it so callously.

With an effort, she let it go. He was right, they shouldn't ruin their brief time together by arguing. But she knew it wouldn't be the last time they spoke about this and wondered with a sudden sense of foreboding how it would all turn out in the end.

SEVEN

'Hey.'

Rahul looked up from his computer, smiling when he saw Natasha standing at his desk. 'Hey, what's up?' he responded.

'I'm taking a break. Do you want to grab some coffee?'

Rahul hesitated. He still had a lot of work and had planned to go to Padmini's house that night to make up with her. He had grown tired of fighting with her over the last few days.

'I still have this report to finish, and I have plans for today,' he said, apologetically.

'Oh, okay.'

She looked so crestfallen that he had to ask, 'Is everything all right?'

'No, I'm just . . .' She cleared her throat. 'My ex just called me and spent the last fifteen minutes screaming in my ear. I just needed something to take my mind off it.'

She looked so miserable that he didn't have the heart to refuse her. 'Okay, let's make it a quick one,' he said and was pleased at the way her expression brightened.

They walked down to the canteen together and ordered

two cappuccinos. Natasha took a sip and made a face. 'I wish they'd make it a bit stronger,' she grumbled.

'I know,' said Rahul.

'So, seen any good shows lately?' Natasha asked.

'I finally started watching *Mad Men*; it's really good.'

She had recommended the show to him a couple of weeks ago and he had decided to give it a try. Padmini had raised hell when she had found out, complaining that she had recommended the same show to him years ago, but he had never agreed to watch it with her. Rahul couldn't remember her ever mentioning *Mad Men* and couldn't understand what the big deal was, even if she had.

'Yeah, the finale was really good this season,' said Natasha. 'I can't believe I have to wait a year for the next season.'

They had an animated discussion on the merits of the show and Rahul completely lost track of time.

'Shit, it's four already!' he said when he finally looked at his watch. 'I'd better get back, otherwise I'll end up spending the entire night here.'

He was going to be really late to Paddy's tonight, he thought guiltily.

'Sorry, I didn't mean to keep you for so long,' Natasha said, standing up.

'It's cool,' said Rahul.

They began to walk back to the office. 'So, I'm having a housewarming party next weekend. I mean, obviously, I moved months ago, but I haven't had the time to do it till now. It'll be just a few friends. You'll come, right?'

'I'd love to,' he said warmly.

They had reached his desk. Just before he sat down, Natasha

put a hand on his arm. 'Thanks,' she said earnestly. 'I really needed that break.'

'No problem,' he said, and meant it. She looked so much happier just from sitting with him for a while and talking about TV shows. He wished he had that effect on Padmini, too.

———

It was eleven when Rahul reached his girlfriend's house that night. He let himself in, hoping she hadn't already crashed. Luckily, he found her sitting in the living room and working on her laptop.

She was on her feet as soon as she caught sight of him, a look of profound relief on her face. 'I am so sorry,' she said. 'I should have told you about the pregnancy scare.'

'Yeah, you should have,' Rahul said. 'Why didn't you?'

'I panicked,' Padmini said softly. 'I thought you would, too, and I didn't want to deal with that. And we'd been fighting so much . . . I know it's not an excuse. I'm sorry.' She sighed helplessly.

'I guess I can understand that,' he said. 'Let's just go to bed now, okay? I'm tired of fighting about this.'

She ran to him and hugged him hard. 'Thanks for making the effort to come over today even though you have so much work,' she said. 'I was going out of my mind knowing you were so pissed with me.'

He hugged her back and planted a kiss on her forehead. 'You know I would have forgiven you eventually,' he said smiling. 'I always do.'

He had always prided himself on the fact that he knew how

to let bygones be bygones. That was why it annoyed him so much when Paddy brought up Purnima after so many years had passed.

'I love you,' she said.

'Love you too,' he said. 'Now let's go have make-up sex.'

She laughed, her head against his chest. 'You are such a guy! We just had a pregnancy scare and you want to jump right back into bed?'

'Well, we can't really help that,' he said with a wink. 'Unless you want to not do it forever . . . ?'

He paused, horrified at the thought.

'Idiot!' she laughed. 'I've started taking birth control pills.'

He frowned. 'Is that safe?'

'Of course it is,' she said. 'It's very effective. And the best part is, we won't have to use condoms.'

He felt a hot flush of desire as he pictured that. Without another word, he grabbed her hand and tugged her towards the bedroom, closing the door and pulling her into his arms. He kissed her, demanding and urgent, and she responded eagerly, her mouth wet and pliant against his. When she pulled away for breath, his mouth descended to the side of her neck and he tongued the sensitive spot he knew so well, making her moan softly.

He bit down gently and she panted, 'Don't—you'll leave a hickey, I have work tomorrow—'

'So wear a scarf,' he told her.

They made out for a little while, until he was too impatient to wait any longer. 'Come on,' he said pulling her towards the bed.

It was the first time they had ever done this without

protection and the sensation was incredible. It wasn't long before they were both riding the edge of climax, the pleasure coming in a quick burst and ebbing away.

As their breathing slowed, Rahul gently slid off her and lay back on the bed, content and satisfied. Padmini turned on her side and faced him, her eyes warm and affectionate. She took his hand in hers and kissed it gently, and he smiled.

When they fell asleep, her hand was still clasped in his.

EIGHT

The next day, Padmini was on her way to work when she got a call from Aastha. 'Hey,' she said.

'How are you feeling?' Aastha asked.

'Much better,' said Padmini. 'Rahul came over and we worked things out.'

'Finally!' said Aastha, sounding relieved. 'So what happened? Did you have to beg and plead and cry to get him to forgive you?'

'Nothing so soap opera-ish,' said Padmini with a laugh. 'He just said that he understood and that he was tired of fighting.'

'Seriously?' Aastha asked sceptically. 'That's it?'

'Well, yeah,' said Padmini. 'You know what Rahul's like. He only stays angry for so long.'

Aastha was silent for a moment, but Padmini had known her long enough to sense that she had something to say. 'What is it?' she sighed. 'Spit it out.'

'It's just . . . you've been going through hell over this for the last few days, fighting with him, and he was apparently so angry that he refused to take your calls. And then he just decides that he's tired of fighting and that's it? I mean, if he could let it go that easily, why did he have to punish you for so long?'

Padmini knew Aastha meant well, but sometimes her friend could really be ridiculous. 'Aastha, *I'm* the one who messed up,' she said, exasperated. 'I should have told him right when I thought I was pregnant. I'm glad he let it go. I don't want to analyse it beyond that.'

'Sorry,' said Aastha. 'I was just . . . Well, I'm just glad things are okay between you two.'

She didn't sound glad and Padmini wondered why Aastha was sometimes so hard on Rahul. But now was not the time to confront her about it. 'It's cool,' she said. 'By the way, what are we doing for Sameer's birthday? It's on Sunday.'

'Well, at first I thought we should do dinner and a movie, like always,' said Aastha. 'But then I realized we've never actually had a party. Sam has a huge apartment and we should take advantage of that.'

Padmini was surprised at the suggestion. She had always assumed that Aastha couldn't handle a full-fledged party.

'Are you sure you'd be okay with something like that?' she asked.

'I think so,' said Aastha, sounding determined. 'A party in Sam's flat isn't the same as a club and as long as it's not more than twenty people, I think I'll be fine.'

'Well, it's different from what we usually do,' said Padmini, still not entirely convinced. 'I think he'd enjoy it, but only if you're completely okay with it.'

'I will be,' said Aastha. 'I can't always stay in my comfort zone and I know you guys are probably tired of doing the same thing every week. Plus, it would solve the problem of figuring out a birthday present for him. The three of us could pitch in to pay for food and alcohol, and I'll figure out whom to call.' Padmini groaned at the thought. 'He has way too many friends at his office. You'll have to track them all down on Facebook.'

They discussed the logistics for a little longer, until Padmini reached her destination and had to get off the metro. She hung up, promising to call Aastha later in the day.

———

Sameer kneaded his forehead as he listened to Karuna's panicky voice through the static-filled Skype connection on his computer. He knew he should be sympathetic, but he was annoyed. He had called her through Skype because he'd missed her and wanted to see her face, not to have a replay of the same conversation they'd already had half a dozen times.

'—don't know what I'm supposed to do,' she was saying. 'My parents are telling me I have to talk to him again and I really don't want to!'

'So don't,' he said impatiently. 'You don't *have* to do anything you don't want to, Karuna.'

'Don't give me that crap again,' Karuna said harshly. 'You have no idea what it's like. I'm stuck here and this is the only thing my parents ever talk about, and if I don't listen to them they won't hesitate to make my life completely miserable.'

'If you really needed it, I could lend you the money,' Sameer said. 'I mean, in case they cut your allowance—'

'That's not even the point!' she screeched. 'How can you be so fucking—?'

'Well, what the hell do you want me to say?' Sameer interrupted, losing his temper. 'You keep shouting at me, but

I can't do anything to fix this! If you don't have the balls to stand up to your parents, it's not my fault!'

She ended the call and he cursed loudly. He was getting tired of her hanging up every time he said something she didn't like. Perhaps he shouldn't have said it so harshly, but he knew he was right.

The doorbell rang, shaking him from his thoughts. He was surprised to see Aastha there. 'Hey, what are you doing here?'

'Oh, you know, I haven't hung out with you in ages, so I thought we could get some coffee,' she said brightly.

'I'm really not in the mood—'

'Sam, please! I haven't seen you in two weeks.'

He was about to protest again when he thought that Aastha was probably trying to get him out of the house so the others could sneak in his birthday cake. Not wanting to be a spoilsport, he agreed to go with her and even left the key under the doormat so the other two could get in.

They walked down to the CCD nearby and found themselves comfortable seats.

'So how come you're in such a bad mood?' Aastha asked.

'I don't really want to talk about it.'

'Oh, come on,' she wheedled him. 'You know I give good advice.' She smiled sweetly.

He sighed, knowing she wouldn't let it go. 'I had another fight with Karuna. Her parents are making her talk to that Joseph guy on the phone, and she keeps taking out her frustration on me.'

'They're actually making her talk to him regularly?' asked Aastha, frowning. 'That's not good.'

'Well, it's not like she'll say yes to him,' said Sameer. 'Anyway, she has time before she has to give a final answer—he's in the US for two months. If she doesn't want to keep talking to him, she can just tell her parents no—that's what she'll have to do eventually, anyway. But she doesn't seem to have the guts to do that and she got pissed when I pointed it out.'

'Sam, you didn't actually say that to her, did you?' Aastha asked, dismayed.

He didn't answer and she shook her head. 'Look, this is exactly why she's so pissed off!' she said. 'You're making it sound like it's the simplest thing in the world to defy her parents like that. You're taking it for granted that she'll say no to Joseph for your sake and that's not fair.'

'Of course she has to say no!' Sameer exclaimed.

'It's not that easy,' Aastha said. 'Not everyone can have parents like yours, you know. My parents pretend to be all cool and modern, but if I actually dated someone, I know they'd freak. Paddy's probably going to go through the same thing. She'll have to tell her parents about Rahul eventually. And c'mon! Karuna shifted back to Bangalore for her parents' sake. Do you really think she would have the guts to tell them?'

Sameer frowned. Even though he didn't want to admit it, Aastha was making sense. 'Okay, so maybe it's hard,' he acknowledged reluctantly, after a pause. 'I still don't get what she wants me to say about it. I can't really do anything to help her with this.'

'Well, it would help if you avoided telling her she doesn't have the guts to stand up to her parents,' Aastha said. 'Look, just try to be a bit supportive and patient. And you should call her and apologize for yelling. I know you don't want to be fighting with her on your birthday.'

'Yeah, I guess.' Sameer said, sighing. *Why did Aastha always have to be right?* 'You know, you really are a pain in the ass, sometimes.'

She grinned at him. 'You'll thank me for it later.'

Single Conversation

Yeah, I guess,' Sameer said, sighing. 'Maybe it takes a little time to be myself again, you know, normally we a pan in the few somewhere.

She turned at this. 'You'll thank me for it later.'

NINE

Aastha stood against a wall and surveyed the living room with an air of satisfaction. Sameer's birthday party was on in full swing. People in various stages of drunkenness were dancing to the booming music and the chocolate cake she had chosen had been appreciated and gobbled up by everyone.

Sameer's reaction when they had walked into the house earlier that evening had been priceless. He had been expecting a cake, not a party, and had gaped when he saw his living room decorated with streamers and balloons. Aastha watched him as he danced with a group of his office friends and decided this had been an excellent idea.

As for herself, the smell of alcohol and the loud music hadn't brought back any memories of F-Bar. In spite of what she had told Padmini, she *had* been apprehensive about this party and was very relieved to discover that she was capable of enjoying herself in this atmosphere. As long as no one bumped into her unexpectedly, she was fine.

Sameer spotted her and smiled. He broke away from his circle of friends and made his way towards her. 'Are you okay?' he shouted over the music.

'I'm fine!' she said. 'Enjoying yourself?'

'Best birthday I've had in years,' he said, grinning broadly. 'Why are you standing here by yourself?'

'You know I get a little jumpy around people sometimes,' she said with an offhand shrug. When he frowned, she rolled her eyes and reassured him, 'Don't worry about it, I've been having fun. Really.'

He searched her eyes and his expression cleared. 'You seem a little too sober for someone who claims to be having fun,' he said. 'Want me to make you a drink?'

Aastha hesitated. She rarely drank and, when she did, it was never more than a couple of Breezers. But watching from the sidelines was only going to entertain her for so long. Perhaps a little liquid courage would allow her to join the others.

'Okay, guess it wouldn't hurt.'

She followed him towards the kitchen. The place was in a mess, littered with plastic cups, ashtrays and half-empty pizza boxes. 'It's going to be hell to clean this up.'

'Completely worth it,' he said. 'I haven't had this much fun in ages. There is something about having your own party.'

As Sameer mixed her drink, Aastha's gaze drifted again to the living room. She caught sight of Rahul dancing with Padmini and two other girls. Paddy's eyes were closed as she bobbed her head to the beat. She saw Rahul's eye linger a little too appreciatively on the other two girls, and Aastha's lips tightened.

'Here,' said Sameer, handing her the drink.

Aastha took a sip and choked. 'Whoa, that's strong.'

'No, it's not!' Sameer laughed. 'You're just not used to it.'

She was about to respond, but one of his friends burst into the kitchen and called him back to the dance floor. Someone turned up the volume and Aastha could feel the floor vibrate under her feet.

Screw it, she thought and gulped down the drink so fast that it made her eyes water.

Then she strode towards the dance floor, joining the group Sameer was dancing with. He grinned at her and took her by the arm, gently propelling her so that she was standing with her back to the wall. That way there would be less chance of anyone bumping into her by mistake. She gave him a grateful smile and then her body began to move to the beat. The alcohol was making her muscles feel loose and relaxed, and the music flowed through her.

Maybe she really was getting over that awful night.

Padmini broke away from the group she was dancing with and made her way towards her. 'This really is a great party!' she shouted to Aastha. 'We did a great job organizing it.'

Aastha gave her a thumbs-up sign as she began to dance with a fervour that made the others stare at her in surprise.

'Dude, are you drunk?' Paddy asked and Aastha winked, smiling. She didn't know if she was drunk, but it had been a long time since she had felt this uninhibited and free.

'I just gave you one drink!' Sameer seemed to emerge from nowhere, an amused grin on his face.

Aastha ignored him. Her eyes fell on Rahul again and she glared when she saw how close he was dancing to one of the girls in the group. She sensed Padmini's gaze and turned to look at her. 'What?' she asked.

'Why don't you like Rahul?' Padmini said abruptly.

'I think you deserve better than Rahul,' Aastha said a little too loudly, just as the music stopped. Her words nearly echoed through the room. There was a sudden silence.

Sameer and his friends stared at her in surprise, and she flushed. Paddy, looking angry, stomped back to Rahul.

'You really are drunk,' Sameer said. 'This is going to bite you in the ass tomorrow.'

'I'm right, though,' Aastha said with more conviction than she felt. The sense of exhilaration that had filled her earlier was slowly fading as another fast-paced Bollywood song began to play.

Sameer shook his head, but didn't reply. Suddenly, Aastha didn't feel like dancing any more.

'I'm going to lie down,' she mumbled, heading for the bedroom.

She sat up, rubbing her face tiredly. There were two girls she didn't know sleeping on the bed beside her and two more on a mattress on the floor. She carefully made her way out of the room.

She stopped when she saw Padmini sitting at the dining table, sipping a cup of coffee. Awkwardly, she seated herself at her friend's side.

'I'm really sorry, Paddy,' she said quietly. 'That was a shitty thing to say.'

'Yeah, it was,' said Padmini evenly, 'especially in front of so many people. Everyone was talking about it after you left. Rahul was really embarrassed.'

She hung her head for a moment. 'I was drunk,' she said. 'I'm sorry.'

'You meant it, though,' said Padmini, her voice hard. Then she sighed and conceded, 'I should never have asked you that in front of everybody. I guess I was drunk, too.'

'It's not that I don't like him,' Aastha hastened to clarify. 'There are times when he's really great, really fun to be around. It's just, you're one of my best friends and I care about you, and I don't like the way he treats you, sometimes.'

'I get that,' said Padmini reluctantly. 'I remember I didn't think Sam was a good fit for Karuna in the first year of their relationship. But the difference is that I got over that and you still haven't, even though we've been dating for four years. Plus, you tend to be really biased. I've started a few of our fights myself. He's not the only one who messes up.'

'I know,' Aastha said. 'I'm sorry. I would never have said it if I'd been in my senses. I'll apologize to him.'

'Do that. I know he won't hold it against you,' Padmini replied. 'It's one of the best things about him. And everyone could see how drunk you were.'

'Yeah,' said Aastha in a subdued voice, still guilty and embarrassed.

Padmini saw her expression and put her hand on her shoulder. 'Don't worry so much,' she said. 'It wasn't your finest hour, but it's not the end of the world.'

Aastha gave her friend a grateful smile. She glanced around the apartment and cringed. 'Maybe we should clean up a bit.'

'Yeah,' Padmini agreed and they both got to work.

Later that afternoon, after all the guests had left and the house had been cleaned, the four friends sprawled haphazardly on Sameer's bed, exhausted by the late night.

Padmini was telling Aastha what she had missed after she'd gone to bed, and the boys, in spite of muttering about 'girls' and 'gossip', listened with interest.

'. . . should have seen how crazy Charu went,' she was saying. 'She did this slutty dance to *Kajra Re* which had all the guys' eyes popping out. Oh, and you know Sam's friend Kshitij?'

'The one who's dating that really thin chick?' Aastha asked.

'Yeah, Simran. You'll never believe this! Simran passed out early—we put her right next to you in Sameer's bed—and then Charu started dancing with Kshitij. And soon they were all over each other, and at one point they locked themselves in the other bedroom! I mean, his girlfriend was in the same house!'

'What an asshole,' said Aastha, shaking her head. 'It sounds like it was a pretty wild party, though.'

'A little too wild,' said Sameer with a groan. 'At one point some of the guys started throwing water at the girls and they all ran in here and locked the door. And then someone pushed the door really hard, so now my lock is broken.'

'Wow, I can't believe I slept through that,' said Aastha.

'Yeah, well, you were really drunk,' said Rahul.

She glanced at him, wondering if this was a taunt, but his smile didn't waver when their eyes met. Paddy had been right. Rahul had readily accepted her apology and wasn't treating her any differently after her drunken outburst. She knew that if their positions had been reversed, she would not have been as gracious and the thought made her feel ashamed.

After a while, Sameer and Rahul dozed off. Padmini buried herself in a set of proofs. Having nothing better to do, Aastha borrowed Sameer's laptop and began to check her Facebook notifications.

She paused when she caught sight of something on her newsfeed. 'Hey, this looks interesting,' she said. 'There's this bear statue display at Central Park in CP. The bears are painted by artists from different countries . . . It's supposed to be running for a couple of weeks. We should go next Saturday.'

'I'd love to, but I'm going home next weekend. It's my parents' 25th anniversary,' Padmini said.

'Oh, wow, congratulate them on my behalf! How long are you staying for?'

'Only a couple of days,' said Padmini. 'Can't really ask for leave with our Goa trip coming up so soon. Which reminds me, I shortlisted a couple of hotels where we could stay. I think we should book one in the next couple of days, before they all get full.'

They discussed the pros and cons of the hotels, looking at the pictures on the internet. An hour later, they had narrowed it down to two hotels. When the other two woke up they discussed it again and finalized all the details.

The following Friday, Rahul drove Padmini to the airport. She was leaving for Bangalore. He had left work early so he could play the dutiful boyfriend and Padmini had been very appreciative.

'I absolutely love your new car,' she said. 'It makes life so much easier.'

'You just like the fact that it saves you cab fare,' he teased.

She laughed.

'So what are you planning to do for the weekend?' she asked him a little later.

'Oh, you know, chill at home,' said Rahul. 'Or maybe Game Night, if Aastha's planning on having one. Although with you gone, it won't be half as much fun,' he said.

She smiled. 'I'll miss you too! Though I am looking forward to seeing Karuna again. It's been way too long. I hope I'll be able to spend the night at her place.'

They pulled up at the terminal. Padmini grabbed her airbag and gave him a quick hug before she got out of the car. 'Bye!' he called after her. 'Text me when you reach home!'

'Will do!'

He would have liked to linger for a little longer and see her off properly, but the irate honking behind him was impossible to ignore. He inched his way towards the exit, annoyed by the amount of traffic.

His phone beeped to signal a text message. It was from Natasha.

Hey ur coming 4 my prty 2moro rt?

He'd completely forgotten about it. Oh, well, it wasn't as though he was doing anything special this weekend. *Of course,* he replied. *Let me know the details.* ☺

TEN

When the doorbell rang, Karuna almost ran down the stairs.

She threw the door open and hugged her friend. 'Hey, it's so good to see you!' she exclaimed. 'I can't believe how long it's been since I saw you last.'

'I know, right?' said Paddy, returning the hug with equal gusto.

'Hello Padmini!' chimed a voice from behind them.

Karuna turned to find her mother smiling warmly at Padmini and she felt a pang. The way she'd been fighting with her parents, she couldn't remember the last time her mother had smiled at *her* like that.

'Hi aunty, how are you?' said Paddy, giving Karuna's mother a quick hug.

'I'm fine. Karuna said you're working in Axe Publishers these days?'

Karuna let the two of them chatter, marvelling at how easily these kinds of conversations came to Paddy. She gave off what Karuna called a 'Sati Savitri vibe' which made most middle-aged women instantly fall in love with her.

'Amma,' she interrupted after a few minutes, 'I'm sure

Paddy wants to come up to my room now.'

'Of course,' her mother responded. 'Will you be staying the night, Padmini?'

'Yes, aunty.'

'Good, good. You enjoy yourself and let me know if you need anything, okay?'

'I will. Thanks, aunty!'

Karuna dragged her friend up the stairs. 'Dude, seriously, why is my mother so in love with you!' she grumbled.

'It's a gift, I guess,' said Padmini. 'My own mother isn't nearly as impressed with me, if that's any consolation.'

'So what's been up with you?' asked Karuna.

'Oh, nothing much,' said Padmini casually. 'Having a decent phase with Rahul after the whole pregnancy scare drama.'

'The whole *what*?!'

'Oh, sorry, I forgot I didn't tell you about that.'

Karuna listened with wide eyes as Padmini recounted the incident. 'How come you didn't tell me any of this?' she demanded as soon as Paddy had finished.

'You were going through a rough phase at home,' said Padmini. 'Speaking of which, how's the marriage situation? Are they still making you talk to Joseph regularly?'

'Once every few days,' said Karuna. 'I should never have agreed to that first phone call.'

'Is the guy nice, though?' Paddy asked.

'Really nice—that's the worst part.' Karuna sighed. 'He's really smart. I'll show you his picture on Facebook, he's not bad-looking. If I weren't dating Sam, I might actually have considered this.'

'And how's Sam been about the whole situation?'

'At first he was a bit of a jerk about it, but I think Aastha talked some sense into him. He's being quite supportive these days. He keeps telling me there's no point in my panicking about it till Joseph comes back from the US—'

'Which is true,' Padmini pointed out.

'I know, but the problem is, I feel I'm leading Joseph on.' Karuna was so glad to be getting this off her chest; Paddy was one of the few people she trusted enough to tell this much. 'We're talking every few days and I'm scared he's already getting attached.'

'I hadn't thought of it like that,' said Paddy, a bit alarmed. 'Can't you, I don't know, be a bit terse and cold in your conversations?'

'You know I suck at acting,' Karuna said helplessly. 'And he's from the same school, you know? So we talk a lot about our old teachers and stuff. I don't know how to be all non-responsive and bitchy.'

'Can't you just tell him about Sameer?' Padmini asked.

'And if it gets back to my parents?' Karuna countered. 'I would be beyond screwed.'

'Would it really be such a disaster if your parents found out?' asked Padmini. 'You are going to marry Sam, eventually. So you'll have to tell them at some point.'

Karuna sat back, surprised. She had become so accustomed to keeping Sameer a secret from her parents that this hadn't even occurred to her.

'How would they react?' Padmini pressed her.

Karuna thought about it for a moment. 'Well, first they'd freak out 'cause he's not a Mallu,' she said. 'But at least he's

Catholic, so I'll be able to give that as an argument. If I tell Amma first, she probably won't react that badly and she'll try to help me convince Appa. And, you know, he *is* from Stephen's, and he's earning well, so it's not like he's a bad match from their perspective.'

'Then it's clear, just do that,' Padmini said.

Karuna shook her head and said wryly, 'But they'll want to meet his parents first thing if I manage to convince them, and formalize it.'

'And you think Sameer wouldn't be ready for that?'

'I don't know,' said Karuna. 'I . . . we've never really talked about that.'

'Seriously?' Padmini asked incredulously. 'After so many years of dating?'

'I don't know, I guess neither of us really wanted to get into it,' said Karuna. 'Have you talked about it with Rahul?'

'A couple of years ago,' said Padmini. 'I was trying to figure out whether I should go abroad for my MA or stay back in Delhi and I asked him how serious we were—'

'Wait, you stayed in Delhi for his sake? You never told me that!'

'I didn't tell anyone. I knew how everyone would react if I told the truth,' Paddy said. 'But it wasn't like I made a huge career compromise for his sake. Stephen's is an excellent college for a postgrad degree, and I have a job I like on more days than I hate it. I'm happy. In a few years, I'll tell my parents about him and we'll probably get married.'

Paddy sounded so sure of herself, Karuna was a little jealous. She and Sameer had never had that kind of practical discussion, although she had always considered it a given that they'd still be together in the distant future. She knew he did too.

Maybe she *should* talk to Sam about it, she thought. Padmini was right; it *was* surprising that they hadn't already had the discussion after so many years of dating. But, well, it wouldn't be a good idea to spring it on him . . .

'Earth to Karuna,' said Padmini, breaking her out of her thoughts.

'Sorry,' Karuna said. 'I was just thinking that your life sounds really sorted.'

'Not that sorted,' said Paddy. 'The amount Rahul and I have been fighting this year is ridiculous. You never know, maybe we will end up breaking up.'

But the way she said it, Karuna could tell she couldn't really imagine that happening. 'I doubt it,' she said. 'You guys are like an old married couple. You fight, but you always make up because breaking up isn't an option.'

'Thank you, that sounds *so* romantic,' said Padmini.

Their conversation turned to other topics and they spent the rest of the night gossiping about mutual friends as they snacked on chips and chocolate. The next morning, when Padmini bid her goodbye, Karuna was feeling a lot better.

———

Later that week, Karuna was lying in bed and trying to study for an upcoming test. She was just finding her focus when her mother knocked on the door. 'Karuna, can I talk to you for a minute?'

Karuna closed her book and sat up. 'Sure,' she said warily.

Her mother sat down beside her. 'I wanted to ask you about Joseph,' she said. 'You've talked to him a few times now. What do you think of him? Is he——?'

'I don't like him,' said Karuna.

'Why?' she asked.

'What does it even matter?' Karuna asked angrily. 'If I say I hate him, you're still going to force me to keep talking to him, aren't you?'

'Mind your tone,' her mother said sharply. When Karuna didn't respond, she sighed. 'I know the last few weeks have been . . . difficult, but we only want what's best for you,' she said softly. 'He's well educated and from a very good family. You could be really happy with him. I don't understand why you're refusing to even consider it!'

Karuna was silent. Ever since Padmini had suggested it, she had been thinking about telling her mother about Sameer. She didn't want her father to know just yet, but maybe her mother wouldn't react that badly. Maybe if she told her the truth, she would understand why she didn't want to marry Joseph and stop pushing her so much.

'If I told you something, would you promise not to tell Appa?'

'Depends on what it is.'

Karuna shook her head. 'No, forget it.' This had been a stupid idea; of course her mother wouldn't make a promise like that, and she really couldn't face another blow-up from her father.

'Karuna, what are you talking about?' her mother asked. 'What don't you want your father to know?'

'Never mind, just forget I even——'

Her mother's eyes narrowed. 'Is there someone you're going steady with?'

Karuna wanted to deny it, but the words stuck in her throat. She cursed herself for her stupidity. Her mother wasn't completely clueless; of course she would put two and two together.

Her mother took her silence for confirmation. 'Who is he?' she demanded. 'Is he a Hindu? What—?'

'Amma, breathe,' Karuna interrupted her mother's frantic questions. 'His name is Sameer Mascarenas and he's a Goan Catholic,' she said. 'He's from St Stephen's College. I met him through Padmini. He works for RTS Enterprises, doing market research and he's earning quite well. His family is quite rich, too.'

She hated talking about Sameer as if he was a business investment, but she knew she would have to market him that way to her parents if she were to have any hope of their approval. Her mother was nowhere near satisfied, though. 'How long have you been going around?' she asked.

Karuna hesitated. If she told her mother the truth, she would be furious. 'We've been friends since college,' she said cautiously. 'But we haven't been dating that long.'

'Then call it off,' her mother said firmly. 'There's no need to jeopardize—'

'Are you kidding me?' Karuna exclaimed, outraged. 'You're the one who asked me why I'm not keen on Joseph and this is what you say when I actually tell you the truth? My relationship with him is serious, Amma. Even in college, we were interested in each other, even if we weren't actually dating. That's why I don't want to marry Joseph.'

'But he's Goan,' her mother said, her forehead creasing with distaste. 'And we know Joseph's parents very well; they're very decent and educated—'

Oh, for heaven's sake. 'So are Sameer's parents!'

'Karuna, you know it's not me you have to convince,' she replied. 'Your father won't approve of this. And even if you can convince him, he'll insist on meeting his parents and then, after that, you'll have to get engaged to him immediately.'

'But *why?*' Karuna asked, even though she had expected this. 'If you can just help me convince Appa that I don't want to marry Joseph—'

'Absolutely not! I can't do that without telling him why. You can't be allowed to continue with this boy as if nothing has changed.'

'You know I can't marry Joseph, I just *told you* I'm in love with someone else—'

'Karuna, I can't risk our relatives finding out about this!' her mother exclaimed. 'If people start talking about how you were going around with a boy in Delhi, you won't be able to find a respectable match anywhere!'

'I don't care about that!' said Karuna, almost in tears. 'You tell me, what am I supposed to do?'

'Think about whether you're so sure about your choice that you can safely disregard your parents' wishes,' said her mother. 'And then if you are sure, if you think it'll be worth all the trouble and the tears, then you can tell your father about Sameer. But you'll have to be prepared to marry him. So whatever you do, please be sure.' With that she walked out of the room, leaving Karuna in a state of turmoil.

Why had she never thought about this? She had always known that her parents would start looking for matches for her soon after her postgraduation, but she'd been so madly in love with Sameer that she had swept it under the rug. She hadn't been prepared for how quickly they would find a good match for her, but that was no excuse. She should have seen this coming a long time ago.

She lay in bed, her books completely forgotten as she tried to figure out what she was going to do.

ELEVEN

Padmini's heart was singing with happiness. After planning the trip for months, she was finally on her way to Goa! One week of sunshine and beaches and shopping with the people she loved best.

She stared out of the airplane window, watching cities and towns pass by in miniature. It was for the first time in her life that she was flying with her own money and she wanted to enjoy every second of it.

'I can't believe we're actually going to Goa after talking about it for so long,' said Rahul, who was sitting beside her.

'I know!' Padmini said, grinning. 'And I already spoke to Aastha—we're getting one of the rooms to ourselves for at least a couple of nights. She and Sam can share.'

She glanced over at Aastha and Sameer, who were sitting across the aisle from them. The two were deep in conversation, their expressions unusually serious. Paddy wondered what they were talking about. They both got so wrapped up in each other sometimes, it was as if they were shutting the entire world out.

'I wish they could share rooms for the entire trip,' said

Rahul, calling her attention back to him. 'I don't suppose you could ask—'

'How would you like it if I shared the room with Sam for a whole week while you were in another city?' she countered. 'He does have a girlfriend, you know.'

'Oh, please, it's *Aastha*,' said Rahul. 'She's like a saint on her best days; there's no way she'll let anything happen.'

Padmini didn't like his tone. 'Don't be mean,' she said. 'There's nothing wrong with having principles.'

'I didn't say there was,' said Rahul. 'But she takes it too far, sometimes. It's as if she thinks she has the right to judge other people's mistakes because she's so sure she'd never make them herself.'

That actually had more than a grain of truth to it. She knew that Rahul had forgiven Aastha for her comment at Sam's party, but he wasn't a saint any more than Aastha was. Even though he was making sure that he treated her as if nothing had changed, Padmini knew he hadn't forgotten about what she had said.

'Remember our trip to Nainital?' she asked, changing the subject.

'You mean the one where you insisted on staying in the room all day?' Rahul asked dryly. 'We barely did any sightseeing—it was ridiculous!'

'I made it worth your while, didn't I?' she said. 'Besides, that was in college. It wasn't like I could sneak you into my hostel room for . . . you know.' Her face burned as she realized they could easily be overheard by their fellow passengers.

Rahul laughed at her and placed an arm around her shoulders. 'You really have a one-track mind, you know that?' he said affectionately.

'Like you're any better,' she grumbled, nestling against him.

As she closed her eyes and rested her head against his shoulder, a feeling of contentment washed over her.

———

Across the aisle, Aastha studied Sameer with concern in her eyes. She had sensed something off about his mood all morning. While the rest of them had been animated and bubbling with excitement at the prospect of their holiday, Sameer had seemed preoccupied and distant.

'Hey, what's eating you?' she asked softly. When he didn't respond immediately, she asked, 'Sam?'

He blinked and came back to himself. 'Sorry. What?'

Aastha frowned. 'I was just asking you if everything is okay,' she said. 'I can tell something's bothering you.'

'Nothing's bothering me,' said Sameer. When Aastha just stared at him, he sighed. 'Okay, fine. It's just that Karuna's been kind of strange lately on the phone.'

'You're fighting again?' Aastha asked.

'No, not fighting,' said Sameer. 'She just doesn't seem to have that much time for me. I mean, she's not ignoring my calls or anything, but when we talk on the phone, it's almost as if she has too much on her mind to really respond properly. It's just . . . weird.'

'Well, she's going through a lot of shit at home,' said Aastha reasonably. 'And with her next set of actuarial exams coming up, of course she'd be under a lot of stress. She must be really busy with the coaching classes and all the mock tests they make them do . . .'

'It's not that,' Sameer insisted. 'I mean, of course the exams and the coaching are hell, but that never came in the way of us talking before, you know. Sure, sometimes she'd be too tired, but then she'd tell me that and we'd hang up. I feel like there's something *wrong* and she's not telling me what it is.'

'Why does she need to *tell* you something's wrong?' Aastha asked incredulously. 'You already know there is! Her parents are trying to marry her off to someone else.' She paused as a thought struck her. 'Maybe that has finally sunk in and that's what's bothering you so much.'

But Sameer shook his head dismissively. 'No, it's something else, I'm sure of it.'

Aastha wondered, not for the first time, why he wasn't taking this more seriously. It was almost as if he couldn't even consider the idea that Karuna might actually marry Joseph. But Aastha had seen two of her cousins go through the same situation a few years ago and, after all the arguments and the drama, they had both succumbed to the pressure and married the guys their parents had picked. She knew there was a very real chance it could happen to Karuna, too, and Sameer wouldn't even see it coming if it did. She was very tempted to tell him so, but she bit her tongue, knowing it wouldn't do any good.

'I'm sure, whatever it is, she'll tell you when she needs to,' she said instead.

'Guess you're right,' said Sameer. 'I'm probably just overreacting.'

But he continued to look troubled, no matter how much Aastha tried to cheer him up.

———

'Okay, this place is awesome!' Sameer declared.

Rahul looked around the spacious hotel room which contained a double bed covered with crisp white sheets, a very comfortable-looking sofa set and, best of all, a small balcony which overlooked the beach in the distance.

'It really is,' he agreed.

'Paddy is amazing,' Sameer said appreciatively. 'How did she manage to find a place like this on our budget? I was expecting something a lot more functional.'

Rahul laughed. Sameer's definition of 'functional' was very different from that of most people. 'I'm sure Paddy will appreciate the praise,' he said. 'Is it okay if I take this side of the bed?' He indicated the side closer to the door.

'Sure,' said Sameer carelessly, flopping down on the other side.

Rahul pushed his suitcase against a wall and went out into the balcony. The weather was a little muggy, but the sea breeze was strong. He inhaled the faintly fishy smell and smiled happily.

Sameer joined him a few minutes later, looking at the busy street below them and the grey strip of sea in the distance. 'I can't wait to go for a swim,' he said. 'We should go today if we can.'

'That'll depend on how long the girls take to settle in,' said Rahul.

'Do you and Paddy want the room tonight?' Sameer said, changing the subject. 'You can have it as often as you want; just say the word. Aastha and I would be totally cool sharing.'

Remembering Padmini's words earlier that day, Rahul couldn't help but be surprised. 'Really?' he asked.

'Of course,' said Sameer. 'Why wouldn't we?'

'Nothing, we just thought Karuna might have an issue with you sharing a room with Aastha,' said Rahul. 'I know Paddy would have a problem with it.'

'Karuna's completely chilled about things like that,' said Sameer. 'She knows Aastha's just a friend.'

'You're really lucky she's not possessive,' said Rahul, wishing Padmini could be that easy-going.

'Well, I've never given her reason to be,' said Sameer, and although his tone hadn't been pointed, Rahul was abruptly reminded of Purnima.

'And I always tell her if I'm sharing a room with Aastha, or anyone else,' Sameer added.

Rahul remembered, with a twinge of something like guilt, that he had still not told Paddy that he had gone to Natasha's party the previous weekend, or that he had ended up spending the night there. He knew he should have told her, but she would have made such a fuss.

'You're only able to do that because you know she won't freak,' he remarked to Sameer before he could stop himself and then coloured when he realized how plainly he'd just revealed himself.

Sameer raised his eyebrows. 'I've always thought that Karuna doesn't freak *because* I tell her everything,' he said in a deliberately offhand tone, and then changed the subject. 'Shall we go find the girls? I want to see if their room is as good as ours.'

'Sure,' said Rahul.

The girls' room was only four doors from theirs. Sameer knocked and Aastha let them in with a bright smile. 'Hey,' she said. 'We were just about to call you; we want to go to the beach.'

'Sounds good,' said Sameer, glancing at his watch. 'We have at least a couple of hours before it gets dark. The rooms are really nice, by the way. You did a great job.'

'Thanks, Sameer,' said Padmini, looking pleased.

They made their way to the beach, which was fairly deserted. The sun was hotter than they had expected, so none of them wasted much time before diving into the refreshingly cool water.

Aastha and Rahul weren't very good at swimming, and didn't venture too far out of the shallow water, but Padmini and Sameer took to the water like fish. Aastha treaded the water close to the beach and stared after them, a little worried as they became smaller and smaller in the distance. Thankfully, it didn't take them long to return, and Sameer started a huge water fight which left them with stinging eyes and flushed faces. They stayed at the beach till it got dark and then reluctantly made their way back to the hotel.

Aastha was feeling happier and more relaxed than she had in weeks, and she barely noticed the sand particles in her clothes and hair. She could already tell this was going to be a wonderful holiday.

That night, Sameer slept in Aastha's room so that Rahul and Paddy could have some privacy. Exhausted from a long day, they both crashed early.

She woke two hours later to the sound of someone frantically knocking at the door. Sameer stirred beside her, muttering about how late it was. 'Who's there?' Aastha called.

'It's Paddy.'

Aastha opened the door and was shocked to see that her friend was crying. 'Hey, what happened?' she exclaimed, pulling her into the room and flicking on the tube light.

'Rahul spent the night at Natasha's last weekend,' Padmini said, distraught. 'I read his messages—I can't believe he *lied* to me—'

'Wait, what?'

But Paddy was crying too hard to explain, so Aastha concentrated on trying to comfort her. 'Here, sit down.'

Padmini collapsed on the sofa, her face in her hands. Aastha sat down next to her and rubbed her back, trying to calm her down. Sameer eyed Padmini with concern and looked at Aastha questioningly. She grimaced and tilted her head towards the door, shooting him an apologetic look.

He nodded his understanding and left the room quickly, heading back to his own for the remainder of the night. Aastha turned her attention back to Paddy, whose weeping had become a little quieter. 'What exactly happened?' she asked. 'What do you mean he spent the night at her place?'

'She had a housewarming party last weekend and she invited him,' said Padmini shakily. 'Before I left for Bangalore, I asked him about his plans for the weekend and he said he didn't have any. He said he'd forgotten about it and that she'd texted him after I'd left, but even if that's true, he should have told me when he remembered.'

'Yeah, he should have,' said Aastha. She was furious on her friend's behalf. 'Bullshit, he forgot about it. He was obviously lying to you.'

'I can't believe he stayed the night there,' Padmini said, heartbroken. 'He's such a fucking asshole!'

'There were other people there, right?' said Aastha.

'Yeah, but I keep thinking about Sam's party, about Kshitij and Charu . . . fuck, I'm gonna be sick.'

She clapped a hand over her mouth and hurried to the bathroom. Aastha followed her, watching with growing alarm as her friend retched repeatedly into the toilet. 'You can't be falling sick again,' she muttered.

Padmini inhaled deeply and straightened. 'I'm not sick, I'm just pathetic,' she croaked self-deprecatingly. She flushed the toilet and moved to the sink, washing her face and rinsing her mouth.

'What do you mean?' Aastha asked.

Padmini turned to face her. 'I figured it out after the whole pregnancy scare,' she said. 'When we were fighting, I kept throwing up for days. But when we made up, I was better immediately.'

'Wait, you're saying this is a psychological thing?' asked Aastha, appalled.

'Yeah,' said Padmini. 'What the hell is wrong with me? This is like a new level of screwed up.'

'It'll be fine,' said Aastha, though she wasn't sure whom she was trying to convince. 'This only started happening recently, right? I'm sure it'll go away.'

'I don't even care about that so much,' said Padmini tiredly, leaning against the bathroom wall. 'I just can't believe Rahul would lie like this. And he won't even admit he's wrong, you know? He said if he had told me, I would have freaked out.'

'With good reason!' Aastha exclaimed. 'What kind of excuse is that?'

'I know,' said Padmini. 'I don't think he actually cheated on me, but he definitely likes her. I've told him a hundred times to cut her out of his life, to stop responding to her messages, but he just *refuses*. He says she's a friend and he can't be that rude. But he doesn't even mention me in front of her—I don't think she even knows he has a girlfriend.'

'Paddy, you can't put up with that,' said Aastha. 'And what about her? Isn't he misleading her too?'

'I don't give a fuck about that bitch,' said Padmini harshly. 'I can't do this any more. I'm not going to speak to him until he agrees to stop talking to her.'

'Good for you,' said Aastha. 'Tomorrow we can chill in here. If we go out, it won't be with Rahul. You just wait, he'll come around after a few days of you not talking to him.'

Padmini looked stricken. 'This stupid fight is going to ruin the vacation for you and Sameer,' she said.

'Don't be ridiculous,' said Aastha. 'Like I'm going to let *Rahul* come in the way of my enjoying Goa. I've been looking forward to this for way too long.'

Padmini gave her a faint smile. 'Thanks, Aastha,' she said. 'I can't believe we had this entire conversation in the loo."

Aastha let out a snort of laughter. 'Come on, let's get some sleep,' she said. 'You look like you are totally zonked and so am I.'

TWELVE

Two days later, despite all her resolutions, Padmini did give in a little. After receiving yet another text from Rahul pleading with her to just *talk* to him, she jumped off her bed and marched to his room before Aastha could say a word in protest. She banged on his door loudly, furious with him and herself for not having the willpower to give him the silent treatment as she had planned.

Sameer opened the door, took one look at her face, and beat a hasty retreat. She was too angry to even feel bad about the fact that she was chasing him out of the room again.

She marched up to the bed where Rahul was sitting and stood directly in front of him with her hands on her hips. 'You wanted to talk?' she snapped.

He gaped at her, speechless, and she lost what remained of her patience. 'What the fuck is wrong with you, Rahul?' she ranted. 'You call me here and you don't even—'

'I'm sorry,' he interrupted, raising his hands in a placating gesture. 'You caught me off guard. I just wanted to say I'm sorry about the party. You're right, I should have told you.'

'Are you going to stop talking to her?' she demanded.

'Paddy, look, I can't, okay? No, wait—' He grabbed her by the elbow as she tried to walk away. 'She's my friend and she also works with me! Think of what you'd do if it were someone in your office. You know it's not possible to just stop talking to someone like that.'

'You need to fix this!' she turned around and shouted. 'You can't just say sorry and expect me to trust you!'

'You lied to me, too!' he snapped. 'About the pregnancy scare. And I forgave you, didn't I?'

She couldn't believe he was throwing that back in her face. 'Fuck you!' she said tersely, wrenching her arm out of his grip violently and striding towards the door.

'Pads, wait, I'm sorry,' he exclaimed, rushing past her to block the door. 'I shouldn't have said that. Look, I just . . .' He shrugged his shoulders with a helpless look on his face. 'What do you want me to do, here? You know I can't stop talking to her, not unless I quit my job.'

Padmini wanted to yell at him, telling him to do just that, but reason intervened. She sighed, frustrated with herself for making yet another concession. 'Fine, don't stop talking to her,' she said through gritted teeth. 'But you need to tell her you have a girlfriend, Rahul. I've had it with your refusing to mention me in front of her.'

Rahul's lips thinned. 'You know I don't try to keep it from her on purpose,' he retorted. 'It just never comes up!'

'Then you *bring* it up,' she said, disgusted by the excuse. 'And you'll do it first thing after we get back.'

'Can't you *see* how awkward that would be?' Rahul pleaded. 'It'll be like I'm trying to make a point. As if she's trying to come on to me and I'm trying to warn her off, or something.'

'That is *exactly* what you'd be doing, yeah,' said Padmini stubbornly.

'But it's just so weird!' Rahul exclaimed. 'What, am I just supposed to go to work on Monday and be all, "Beeteedubs, I have a girlfriend"? Out of nowhere?'

'Have you ever heard of subtlety?' Padmini asked in disbelief. 'Can't you just say, "I had a great trip to Goa with my girlfriend", or—you know what? I am *not* doing this for you. You figure out how to tell her and I don't *fucking* care if you feel awkward about it.'

There was a long silence and then Rahul sighed. 'Fine,' he said. 'I'll tell her. I just don't understand why you can't trust me. I'm not saying this to hurt you, but you've made mistakes too and I never acted like this.'

'I know I've made mistakes,' said Padmini. 'But this is different and you know it.'

She was glad he didn't ask her how it was different, because she didn't want to tell him the truth—that she had never been able to trust him fully after Purnima. Last time, she had tried to give him the benefit of the doubt, had ignored the voice which was telling her that Rahul and Purnima were getting too close to each other too quickly, and she had ended up regretting her failure to intervene. This time, even if it seemed irrational and paranoid, she was going to trust her instincts.

As Rahul moved away from the door with a look of resignation on his face, Padmini felt all the fight drain out of her. She followed him and sat down beside him on the bed. For a long moment, neither of them said anything.

Even though they had technically made up, Padmini didn't feel as if everything was fine again. She could see that he resented her for not trusting his word. She herself was feeling hurt by his continued insistence on talking to Natasha. Padmini was more convinced than ever that he had a crush on her, even if he hadn't admitted it to himself. For now, though, they had reached a stalemate. Padmini could only hope it would last.

Sameer was irritated. He had left his cell phone behind when he'd rushed out of his room. Even though an hour had passed, he wasn't sure it was safe to go back. He hadn't spoken to Karuna since the previous morning and he really wanted to talk to her.

'You know, I can't believe how much they've been fighting,' he complained to Aastha. 'Why'd they have to do this on our Goa trip?'

'It's not exactly Paddy's fault,' she retorted. 'Rahul's the one who lied to her. I just hope she has the sense not to back down as easily as she usually does.'

'I don't care who backs down from what, I just hope they both get over themselves,' said Sameer wearily. 'We haven't been down to the beach in two days.'

'No one stopped you from going,' said Aastha half-heartedly.

'And who was I supposed to go with?' he scoffed. 'Rahul wasn't exactly in the mood and you've been sticking to Paddy like a leech.'

Aastha looked guilty. 'I didn't mean to ditch you. I've just been really worried about Paddy. It—she's—she doesn't take fighting with Rahul very well.'

'It's cool, Aastha,' he said. 'It's not you I'm bugged with.'

'Still,' she began, but was interrupted by a knock on the door.

Sameer breathed a sigh of relief when the door opened to show Rahul and Padmini. Neither of them looked very cheerful, but at least they didn't seem like they were two inches away from killing each other.

'I take it you've made up?' Sameer said.

Rahul gave him an apologetic look. 'Yeah. Sorry, man, we didn't mean to chase you out.'

'It's cool, as long as you're not fighting any more,' said Sameer. 'We're going to the beach first thing tomorrow, by the way.'

'That sounds great,' said Padmini with a smile and Rahul brightened at the prospect.

Sameer left them with Aastha and walked back to his room to find his cell phone. He dialled Karuna's number. 'Hey, Sam,' she greeted him dully.

'You sound exhausted,' said Sameer.

'I haven't been getting a lot of sleep lately,' she admitted.

'Studying?' he asked. Her next set of exams was coming up in a month's time.

'No,' she said. 'I just have a lot on my mind, I guess.'

'The whole marriage thing?' he said, surprised even though he shouldn't have been. He knew she was under a lot of pressure from her parents, but he hadn't thought it would affect her sleep.

'Kind of,' she said evasively. 'Sam, can I ask you something?'

'Of course,' he said, a little alarmed.

'Where do you see us five years from now?'

'Hopefully, I'll have an MBA degree by then and be working at a really good company,' he said, confused by the question. 'And you'll have finished your actuaries, so you'll be a proper analyst—'

'Sam, I didn't mean our careers,' she interrupted. 'I mean, do you still see us together?'

'Of course I do!' he said in surprise. 'Don't you?' When she didn't reply immediately, his stomach clenched with fear. Aastha had told him not to just *assume* Karuna would refuse Joseph and he had shrugged her off. But now Karuna was hesitating to confirm something he had always taken completely for granted and he wondered if Aastha was right.

'Karuna, you're not thinking of saying yes to Joseph, are you?' he asked urgently. 'I know you're under a lot of pressure, but you can't—'

'It's not that,' she cut in hastily and then stuttered. 'I . . . I was just checking if you felt the same way. I can't even—it's been so difficult, Sam, I don't—'

His worry increased when she started crying. 'Hey, it's okay, Karuna,' he said. 'Don't cry.'

'I *hate* having to talk to him,' she said shakily. 'I feel like we're becoming friends and that's the last thing I want. And I don't want to lead him on, Sam, I really *don't*, but if I stop talking to him my parents will kill me. I feel like I'm cheating on you every time I talk to him—'

'Hey, you're not, Karuna,' he said, shaken by her distress. 'You can't think like that. Look, if it's killing you this much, say no to marrying him and to hell with what your parents say. Whatever it is, it can't be worse than how you're feeling now.'

'Yeah, it can,' she sobbed. 'You don't know what it's like. Even now, they're so disappointed in me for fighting them so much. I'll hurt them so much if I refuse outright. They're my *parents,* you know? Before I came to Delhi, I was a model daughter. I topped school; I never did anything they didn't want me to. They were so *proud* of me, Sam. And then I came to college, and everything changed. I made friends, and I met you, I started lying to them when we went out late; and before I knew it, I had a whole life in Delhi they knew nothing about. And then I came back home, and my parents saw how different I was, and they didn't know what to do with me. I don't want to hurt them more than I already have.'

Sameer had no idea what to say. He had not realized how badly this had been affecting her, probably because every time she had brought up her parents, it had ended in an argument. He felt guilty as he realized how insensitive he had been. Aastha was right—he *hadn't* taken this seriously enough. 'We'll figure it out, Karuna,' he said softly.

'Yeah.'

He listened to her cry until she managed to calm herself down. 'I'm sorry, I didn't mean to depress you when you're on holiday,' she said.

'Don't be silly.'

There was a short pause and then he said cautiously, 'We do need to talk about this, though. Figure out what we're going to do.'

'Not now,' she said immediately. 'I don't want to get all upset again.' She hesitated. 'But yeah, you're right. We *do* need to talk when you get back to Delhi, and not just about this. I've been putting it off for too long.'

The words sent a tendril of foreboding down his spine. 'What do we have to talk about?' he asked sharply.

'Don't freak out,' she hastened to assure him. 'It's just not the kind of conversation I want to have over the phone. Can we Skype on Monday night?'

'Yeah, sure,' he said reluctantly.

'I'm gonna hang up now,' she said. 'I should wash my face before Amma calls me for dinner.'

'You do that,' he said. 'I love you.'

'I love you, too.'

Sameer hung up. He was worried, even though she had said he didn't need to be. She had sounded so serious and earnest when she said they needed to talk. His phone beeped and he saw that Aastha had sent him a text.

Going out for dinner—meet us at the entrance in 5.

Okay, he replied.

He tried to shake off his lingering sense of unease and focus on enjoying dinner with his friends, but it was difficult. More than once, he could feel Aastha's concerned gaze resting on him.

After dinner, when they got back to the hotel, Sameer headed straight for Aastha's room. He knew without having to ask that Rahul and Paddy would want to spend the night together, and he was only too happy to get out of their hair. He was only half aware of Aastha rummaging through her suitcase and disappearing into the bathroom to change.

He still couldn't get over how distraught Karuna had sounded on the phone. When she'd poured out her conflicted feelings about her parents, it had come as such a surprise. All through college, she had always referred to them as 'insanely strict' and 'crazy', and he had got the impression that she just didn't care very much about what they thought. He would never have guessed that she would struggle so much with the idea of defying them.

'Hello? Sam?'

Aastha's voice pulled him out of his thoughts. He'd been so preoccupied that he hadn't even noticed when she'd come out of the bathroom.

She was staring at him quizzically.

'What?' he asked.

'Dude, I just called you like three times,' she said. 'Is everything okay? You seemed a little off at dinner.'

He grimaced. Aastha was far too good at reading him.

'Just, you know, relationship crap,' he said, not wanting to elaborate.

'Fight?' she asked.

'Not exactly,' he hedged.

'*Sameer,*' she said.

He sighed, knowing she wouldn't let it go until he told her. 'She's really upset about Joseph. She hates having to talk to him, but she doesn't want to hurt her parents by saying no. She sounded really confused. I guess you were right about the fact that I wasn't taking it seriously enough.'

'That sucks,' said Aastha sympathetically. 'I don't think there's much you can do about it, though, except be supportive. Even that much will make a huge difference. If she knows you're taking it seriously, she'll feel a lot less alone.'

'Yeah, I guess you're right,' said Sameer. He gave her a small smile. 'You know, for someone who hasn't ever dated, you give surprisingly good relationship advice.'

'Thanks,' she said dryly. 'I've had loads of practice with Paddy.'

'That must be like a full-time job,' Sameer said, thinking of the continual state of flux Paddy and Rahul were in. He was glad neither of them ever asked him for advice. 'You must be so glad you're single when you listen to all our shit.'

'Not really,' she said, looking a little sad.

'You want to be in a relationship?' he asked, surprised. She had never given any indication that she was unhappy.

'No, I—it's not that, exactly.' She shrugged and looked away from him. 'It's just that it does get a bit lonely, sometimes.'

'You never told me that,' he said. 'Why don't you try to date someone?'

'It's not like I think about it that often,' she said, trying to shrug it off. 'I'm not some sad little girl waiting for love to find her.'

'Still, you should make more of an effort,' said Sameer. 'You never even try to get to know any of my friends, or Nainika's. How do you expect to find someone if you don't—'

'Sam, what's the point?' she interrupted. 'You know I can't stand it when people get too close.'

'So?' he countered. 'That's not all there is to a relationship.'

'Maybe not,' she said, 'but hand-holding and kissing are kind of essential, aren't they? And then there's me, jumping five miles out of my skin if a guy so much as taps me on the shoulder.'

He hadn't known it was that bad. 'I thought you only hated it when people come up from behind you,' he said.

'That's the worst,' she confirmed. 'And yeah, the rest of it *has* gotten better over time. But I'm still really uncomfortable around most people. I will probably always be.'

Her words left him with a hollow feeling in his chest. How could she just accept it like that, the loneliness of not being able to date anyone, being continually on edge, as if it was an integral part of her life? For the thousandth time over the last few years, he cursed that faceless man for everything he had taken from her.

'Hey, it's fine, Sameer,' she said when she saw the look on his face. 'I honestly don't think about it that often. I have good friends and a job that keeps me fairly busy. I'm not pining for a boyfriend.'

He could see that she was being honest, but he still felt terrible for her.

'Now, can we stop talking about this and play a card game or something?'

'Yeah, okay.'

They played two rounds of rummy before deciding to call it a night.

THIRTEEN

Aastha smiled. In her dreams, she could feel someone's arms around her, pulling her back into something solid and warm. She had never before felt so safe, so loved; and she decided then and there that she never wanted to wake up.

Then the arm across her shoulder seemed to tighten and she felt a comforting weight settle on her legs. Slowly, she opened her eyes. That feeling of contentment and safety didn't go away, and neither did the arms around her. For a moment, she blinked uncomprehendingly in the darkness, wondering whether she was still asleep. Then her eyes swept around the room and awareness began to trickle in.

She was in Goa, in her hotel room. Sameer had played cards with her last night and then they'd gone to sleep. They'd shared a bed, like they'd done so many times in the past, but nothing like this had ever happened before. She could hear his gentle snoring in her ear. Her breathing stuttered.

She looked down and saw Sameer's muscular forearm draped across her chest. She became aware that his leg was hooked around her lower body. And she could feel his . . . his *arousal* against her back. Her breathing sped up and her cheeks burned with embarrassment. This was beyond unacceptable. She needed to get away from him, now, preferably without waking him up.

Even as she thought that, she was ashamed to discover that she didn't want to get away. She should be completely freaked out by this; she knew it was creepy and inappropriate. But she hadn't lost that overwhelming feeling of comfort from his proximity. Her insides twisted with guilt as she tried to shift away from him. As he felt her moving, he pulled her even closer in his sleep, mumbling something unintelligible.

She suddenly became very aware of his chest pressed against her back, his hips and thighs against her legs, his soft breaths tickling the back of her neck. If she moved down just a little, his erection would be pressed firmly against her ass. Against her will, her nipples hardened with arousal.

'Sam,' she said in a faltering voice.

He stirred, but didn't wake up.

Her heart began to pound wildly. She needed to get away from him, now. 'Sameer,' she tried again, louder this time.

'Karuna?' he mumbled against her neck.

Of course he thought he was holding his girlfriend. *'Sameer!'*

He jerked awake with a startled gasp. 'What the——*Aastha*?'

Abruptly, his body shot away from hers. She sat up and scrambled towards the edge of the bed, her chest heaving as if she had just run a marathon.

'Fuck!' he said. 'I was dreaming about Karuna and I must have——in my sleep——I'm *so sorry*. Are you okay?'

When she didn't reply, he cursed and switched on the light. She flinched and turned her face away, suddenly afraid that he would see how aroused she still was.

'Aastha?' he said wretchedly, touching her shoulder.

The warmth of his hand shattered the remains of her composure. Operating on instinct, she flung herself off the bed and rushed into the bathroom, locking the door behind her. In her haste, she had forgotten to switch on the light, but she was in darkness only for a few seconds before Sameer switched it on from the outside. She sank down on the closed toilet seat and buried her face in her hands, trying to calm her breathing.

'Aastha, come out,' Sameer pleaded from the other side of the door. 'I didn't mean to—just please come out, okay?'

'I'm fine,' she said in a raw voice. 'Just go back to sleep.'

'Are you crying?' he asked, alarmed.

She couldn't think, couldn't make sense of anything while he was still talking to her. 'No,' she said in a broken voice. 'I just need a minute. Please, could you go to sleep? I'll be fine.'

'Aastha . . .' He trailed off helplessly.

'*Please*, Sam.'

'If you're sure,' he said, and then his footsteps shuffled away.

Aastha closed her eyes and tried to make sense of what had just happened. What she'd just experienced should have made her terrified and disgusted, but instead she'd felt *aroused*. How could she have reacted that way? She could still feel his body pressed against every inch of her.

She pictured Sameer as she had never pictured him before—the warmth of his smile and his strong wiry body. She thought of him laughing, the earnest look on his face when she gave him advice, the reassuring sound of his voice after she had a nightmare. She had always thought he was good-looking, but had never seen him as anything other than a friend. She had never let herself, because of Karuna. But now, it was as though a switch had been flipped.

It was a long time before she had composed herself enough to dare going back into the room. She was nervous at the thought of sleeping next to Sameer after what had happened, but to her relief, he had moved to the sofa. She saw his eyes flicker open and realized he was awake, but then he closed them again and pretended to be asleep.

She quickly turned off the light and climbed into bed. It was a long time before she could fall asleep again.

Sameer felt exhausted when his eyes opened early the next morning. He had tossed and turned for most of the night, plagued by guilt over what had happened. He knew it had been an accident, but that didn't make him feel any less guilty. It would have been bad enough if it had been any other girl, but for him to have done that to *Aastha* was inexcusable.

Only last night she'd talked about how she couldn't stand it when people touched her and he had ended up *spooning* her. The panic in her voice when she shouted his name had been palpable. He couldn't believe he had done that to her.

He turned and watched her still form on the bed. Her face looked troubled even in her sleep. He wondered if she was having a nightmare—he would never be able to forgive himself if his actions had triggered a flashback.

The weight of his thoughts was becoming oppressive and, eventually, it forced him out of bed. He stepped out on to the balcony and dialled Karuna's number.

She picked up the phone on the third ring. 'Hey, you're up early,' she said.

'Something happened,' he said without preamble. 'I—last night, after you said we had to talk, I kept thinking about you. I spent the night in Aastha's room because Rahul and Paddy wanted the other one. I think I was dreaming about you, because when I woke up, I . . .'

'What?' she prompted him.

'I was holding Aastha,' he said. 'I thought she was you, I think I even said your name when I was half asleep. She freaked out and now I don't know what to do.' He debated telling her that he'd been aroused, but couldn't bring himself to admit that aloud. There was a long silence on the other end and he added a little desperately, 'Please don't be mad.'

'I'm not,' she said finally. 'I mean, I'm not exactly happy about it, the thought of you doing that with someone else is . . .'

'I know,' he said.

'But it was obviously a mistake and I really appreciate the fact that you told me.'

That was it? He let out a relieved breath.

'Aastha freaked out?' she asked.

'Yeah,' he said with a heavy sigh. 'She's not comfortable with people touching her and she woke up to find me—like that. She locked herself in the bathroom and wouldn't come out when I called her. She kept saying she was fine, but I could hear her crying. I ended up sleeping on the couch for the rest of the night.'

'That sucks,' said Karuna, genuinely sympathetic. 'I hope she'll be okay.'

'What if she isn't?' he asked in a rush. 'You know how much she counted on me . . . and now if this—'

'Based on what you've told me about her, I think she'll get over it,' Karuna interrupted. 'Her friends are pretty important to her and I'm sure she knows it was a genuine mistake—she's not going to forget how you were there for her for so many years.'

'Yeah, I guess,' he said a little despondently.

'Cheer up, Sam, it'll be fine,' said Karuna. 'Listen, I gotta go now, it's time for breakfast. We'll talk after you get back, okay?'

'Sure,' he said. 'Bye.'

She hung up.

He stared out at the thin stretch of beach in the early morning light. In spite of Karuna's words of reassurance, he didn't feel better. He stood there for a while before re-entering the room.

He stopped short when he saw that Aastha was awake. She seemed to freeze at the sight of him too.

'I'm so sorry,' he said, taking a step forward. 'For last night, I—'

'Don't,' she said, a little desperately. 'Let's not do this, okay? Please? I'm fine.'

'No, you're not,' Sameer said. 'I need you to understand that—'

'—it was a mistake?' she finished for him. 'I understand that, believe me. And I'm okay . . . really, I am, but I don't want to talk about this. Can't we just pretend it didn't happen?'

His heart sank, but the frantic look on her face prevented him from arguing any further. 'If that's what you want,' he said.

'I do,' she said and then abruptly changed the subject. 'Paddy just texted me and we're going down to the beach in ten. We'll have breakfast after.'

'Sounds good,' said Sameer dully.

She took some clothes from her suitcase and went into the bathroom to change. He almost took advantage of the empty room to do the same, but the thought of her walking out suddenly deterred him. On any other day, he would have just called out and told her he was changing. But everything between them seemed so strained this morning, he didn't know how to talk to her normally.

So he waited for her to come out of the bathroom. She looked exhausted. He wondered whether she had gotten any sleep the previous night. They left the room in an uneasy silence.

When they got to the beach, Rahul and Paddy immediately ran towards the water, splashing around and teasing each other good-naturedly. Sameer was relieved to see them finally back to their normal selves.

Aastha didn't head for the water but sat down near the shore, where the sand was moist and malleable. Idly, she began to dig and pile the sand into a tiny hill, patting it into shape with her hands. Sameer hovered indecisively for a minute before sitting down beside her. He wanted to make things right with her—he hated the loss of their easy companionship—but he didn't know how to.

Her eyes flicked towards him. 'You don't have to wait around for me,' she said. 'I know you love swimming.'

'I'm good,' he said. 'That looks nothing like a sandcastle.'

'Well, I don't have any plastic buckets with me,' she said. 'I'd like to see you do better.'

'Challenge accepted!' he said and she laughed.

For a moment, it seemed as if nothing had changed between

them, as if the previous night had been nothing more than a bad dream. He reached forward, wanting to demolish her sandcastle so he could make a better one in its place, but his hand brushed against hers. She jumped and recoiled as if she'd been burned.

He froze, cut to the quick.

'Sorry, you startled me,' she muttered, refusing to meet his eyes.

He stared at her and wondered how the hell he was going to fix this. Aastha was easily his best friend. No one knew him better than she did and they had always been completely comfortable with each other. The thought of losing that sent a stab of fear through his heart. He wouldn't be able to bear it if he always had to be careful around her, if he couldn't sling an arm around her shoulders when he felt like it, or affectionately smack her arm when she teased him. Suddenly, he couldn't bear to sit there for another second.

'I think I'll go for that swim,' he mumbled and walked away.

———

When Aastha had told Sameer she wasn't pining for a boyfriend, she hadn't been lying. Sure, she felt lonely sometimes, but by and large, she had been reasonably content with her life. Part of that was because she had never actually fallen for anyone. When she had pictured dating someone, it had always been a vague faceless stranger.

But now everything had changed. When she had woken up with Sameer's arms around her, she had felt loved and safe. When he had said Karuna's name, the disappointment had been shockingly acute. In the days that followed, she had tried to act as if nothing had changed, but whenever he was around her, the only thing she remembered was how good it had felt when he had held her.

Her feelings for him made her feel guilty and ashamed. She knew he was madly in love with Karuna and Aastha had always thought she was good for him. Besides, she wouldn't be able to live with herself if she went after another girl's boyfriend.

Where did that leave her? As his friend? Whenever she pictured lounging next to him on a sofa, consoling him after a fight with Karuna, she flinched. She wasn't some tragic self-sacrificing heroine from a mid-90s Bollywood film to be able to pull that off. Besides, no one knew her better than Sameer. He would probably see right through her if she tried to put on an act. But she couldn't tell him how she felt, any more than she could act as if nothing had changed.

The hopelessness of the situation made her last few days in Goa pure torture. She knew that Sameer had probably got some inkling of her feelings by then. She had been acting too strangely for him not to have guessed. There was a wary, guilty look in his eyes whenever they spent time together and, after the incident on the beach, he was very careful not to touch her again.

All in all, they were both glad when the trip was over.

FOURTEEN

On the evening of their return from Goa, Sameer Skyped with Karuna. Her 'we need to talk' speech had been weighing on him for days and he wanted to clear the air between them.

'Hey,' she said, smiling at him through the screen. 'You're back in Delhi?'

'Yeah,' he said.

'Bet you're not looking forward to going back to work tomorrow,' she said sympathetically.

'I am, actually,' he said. 'The Goa trip was a little too eventful, what with Paddy and Rahul constantly at each other's throats, and Aastha . . .' He shook his head and sighed.

'How are things with her?' Karuna asked.

'I don't know,' said Sameer. 'Awkward.'

'I'm sure it'll be okay,' Karuna said vaguely, but she didn't press him further. He could tell she had other things on her mind, so he decided to get to the point.

'What did you want to talk to me about?'

She lowered her eyes so she wasn't looking directly into the webcam. 'I told my mom about you,' she said.

'You what?' he asked, shocked. 'When?'

'A couple of weeks ago,' she said. 'I'm sorry, I know I should have told you before, but it's just been really difficult.'

'What did she say?' he asked.

'She freaked out at first, especially when she heard you didn't have a postgrad degree. But I think she was relieved when I told her you were Catholic, and that you're planning to do an MBA.'

'Well, thank God for small mercies,' he muttered sarcastically. 'I'm glad to hear I'm such a wonderful catch.'

'That isn't helping,' she snapped at him. 'I don't like this any more than you do, but I can't help the way my parents think.'

'Sorry. What about your dad?'

'Haven't told him yet. Mom said I needed to be sure before I did.'

'Sure of what?' he asked.

She hesitated. 'You have to understand, he's going to lose it when he finds out about us. He'll yell at me for going around with you, give me a lecture about how I have no concern for my family's reputation and try to forbid me from seeing you. But he'll probably calm down if he sees that I'm serious about you. If I manage to convince him to accept it, he'll want to meet your parents immediately—'

'I don't have a problem with that,' interjected Sameer.

'—and then he'll want us to get engaged and married within the year,' she finished.

Sameer threw his head back and let out an incredulous laugh. 'Yeah, like that's going to happen.'

'You said you saw us together five years from now,' she said, hurt.

'Wait, you're serious?' he asked in disbelief. 'You want us to get married? *This year?*'

'Why not this year?' she asked, a little desperately. 'We both know we will eventually; we love each other, we could make it work.'

'Have you forgotten that I'm going abroad for my MBA next year?' he asked. 'I'm giving the GMAT at the end of this year and I haven't even started studying yet. I don't even know which university I'm going to.'

'Okay, yeah, I know that,' she said, a pained frantic look in her eyes. 'And I never ever thought I'd ask this of you, I never thought I'd ask you to compromise on something so huge, but my parents are not going to let me say no to Joseph if I don't have a good enough reason. Can't you give the CAT and do the MBA in India?'

The direction the conversation had taken had left Sameer reeling. 'But I don't want to do my MBA here,' he said. 'The CAT is way too competitive. Even if I study my ass off, I won't get into a decent college. You know that.' They had never had this kind of conversation before and only now did he realize how foolish and short-sighted they had been.

'What about a long engagement?' she asked suddenly, catching him off guard again.

'What?'

'If we formalize it, my parents might accept it,' she said. 'We could get engaged, you could go do the MBA, and we could get married when you got back.'

He considered that. It wasn't as bad as getting married that year, but he still had serious misgivings. 'Would your parents be okay with that?' he asked cautiously.

'No,' she said. 'But if I refuse to marry anyone but you, they won't really have a choice.'

Suddenly, he was annoyed. 'Let me get this straight,' he said. 'You're willing to fight that hard to marry me, but you can't just say no to Joseph and deal with the consequences?'

'I have to have a reason to say no to Joseph,' she said. 'What they want, deep down, is for me to get married to someone decent as soon as possible. So I could probably convince them about you, but I can't just say no to Joseph and not give them a reason. Besides, my mom knows about us now. If I say no, she'll know why and she'll tell Appa. There is no way in hell I'll be allowed to keep seeing you.'

Sameer made a frustrated noise. 'You aren't in school, Karuna!' he said. 'You're educated, and you could probably start working tomorrow and earn well enough to support yourself. A lot of people give the actuaries while working. It takes longer, but so what? At least your parents won't be able to walk all over you.'

'It's not that easy,' she said.

He was getting really tired of that line. 'I know,' he snapped. 'Do it anyway.'

Her eyes hardened. 'Do you even know what you're saying? I'm their only child. It would crush them if I walked out on them like that. Could you do that to your parents?'

'I wouldn't have to,' he said before he could stop himself.

She glared at him. 'Yes, thank you, Sameer, I know your parents are a lot more liberal than mine. Yay for them.'

'That's not what I meant and you know it,' he snapped, and then forced himself to pause and inhale deeply. 'This isn't helping.'

'Sorry,' she said, her expression growing more serious. 'Look, are you going to at least *consider* the long engagement idea?' she asked.

'I don't know,' he said. 'Honestly, I never saw myself getting married till I was like, thirty. Maybe even older. Definitely not till my career was completely set.'

Her face went slack with shock. 'Really?'

'Um, yeah. What about you? I mean, if you could decide without your parents being involved.'

'I never really thought about it,' she said. 'But a lot earlier than that. Maybe twenty-six or twenty-seven. Ideally, I'd like to start a family before I turn thirty.'

Shit, he thought dazedly. How could they not have known this about each other after more than five years of being together? He hadn't even thought about when or if *he* wanted to start a family. It was terrifying to be completely in sync with someone for so long and then suddenly find out that they were on completely different pages.

'We should have talked about this ages ago,' she said.

'Yeah,' he agreed, feeling lost.

They were silent for a while, staring at each other. 'Will you at least think about it?' she asked finally.

He really, really didn't want to, but he knew he owed her this much after five years. 'Okay,' he said grudgingly. 'But, Karuna, you need to think about standing up to your parents, too. You can't put this all on me.'

'Yeah, okay,' she said reluctantly.

Obviously, they would both have a lot to think about in the coming weeks.

———

Three days after their return from Goa, Aastha had a nightmare. It was the same one she had always had, about the night in F-Bar and the attack, except that in this one, she couldn't find Sameer. She stumbled around in the flashing strobe lights, her attacker close at her heels, unable to find him no matter where she looked.

She woke up in a cold sweat, gasping for breath. Her hand reached across the bed for her cell phone—the only thing she wanted in that moment was to hear Sameer's voice. But just as her fingers began to dial his number, she stopped herself. She couldn't keep calling him in the middle of the night whenever she had a nightmare. She needed to stop depending on him so much, or she would never get over him.

It was a good hour before she was able to calm herself, and even after that she didn't fall asleep because her thoughts were still racing. The dream had scared her and she wondered what it said about her equation with Sameer. More than anything, she wanted to talk to Paddy about this, but she was worried that she would tell Rahul. The last thing she needed was for the incident to become an open secret in the group.

Besides, Paddy had more than enough on her plate already. Rahul had not yet told Natasha he had a girlfriend and, of course, they were arguing about it every day. Aastha had told her to just stop speaking to Rahul, but she hadn't been able to. It was frustrating to watch. Paddy was slowly destroying herself in what was clearly becoming a suffocating relationship and Aastha felt powerless to help her.

She turned on her side, wondering when her life had become so complicated. It was a long time before she was able to fall asleep again and, when she did, she dreamt of Sameer again.

FIFTEEN

Rahul was fed up. It had been five days since their Goa trip, and he was still completely swamped with all the work he had to catch up on. As if that wasn't enough, Padmini was constantly pushing him to tell Natasha that she was his girlfriend, complaining that he was supposed to have done it days ago. The ultimatum was irritating enough without the added indignity of being held to a deadline, he thought, annoyed.

If only Padmini would trust him . . . they could have avoided all this unpleasantness. Her possessiveness had grown over the years and he knew it was a big reason why they kept fighting. He would never have kept the truth from her in the first place if he hadn't been afraid of her reaction. And now she was being deliberately stubborn, refusing to understand how awkward it would be to pointedly tell Natasha he had a girlfriend.

He sighed and turned his attention to the report he was working on. It was an important one, and had to be sent to the US office by the following day. A G-Talk chat window pinged open on his computer. It was a message from Natasha.

m bored. ☹

i know, he typed back.

coffee break?

sure, he responded immediately. Coffee breaks with Natasha were sometimes the only bright spot in his day.

She emerged from her cubicle across the office and he walked down to the cafeteria with her. 'So, watched any more *Mad Men?*' she asked when they had found a table.

'I watched some in Goa,' he said. He thought of adding 'But my girlfriend wouldn't let me stay glued to the laptop for very long,' but it sounded far too deliberate and pointed.

'I so envy you, getting to go to Goa and all,' she said. 'I wish I had someone to go on a trip with.'

Her expression turned a little sad. Natasha had told him a few weeks ago that her ex-boyfriend had been her whole life when they'd been together, that she had made the mistake of losing touch with many of her friends because she was so hung up on him and, now that it was over, she was very lonely. He thought that was probably why she texted and posted on his wall as often as she did. But when he had tried to explain this to Paddy, she had cynically claimed that Natasha was just playing the damsel in distress.

'Next time, maybe you could come with us,' he said.

He could just hear Paddy's voice in his head, yelling 'Over my dead body!', but he ignored it.

Natasha smiled in response and said, 'I'll hold you to that.'

The next half hour would have passed pleasantly, if not for the fact that he kept trying to think of ways to slip in the information that he had a girlfriend, with little success. They talked about office politics and colleagues, TV shows and the heaps of work they both had to finish. Finally, she asked him about his weekend plans.

'Oh, you know,' Rahul said as casually as he could, 'probably Game Night on Friday at my girlfriend's place.'

There was a momentary flicker in Natasha's eyes, but other than that she didn't react. 'That sounds nice,' she said lightly. 'I'm planning to go for the second *Thor* movie on Saturday.'

He let out a relieved sigh—that hadn't been awkward at all. 'Oh, yeah, it's supposed to be really good,' he said.

'All these superhero movies are too similar,' said Natasha. '*Thor* is probably the only one which actually has a sense of humour. The rest of them are so full of doom and gloom, it's ridiculous.'

'No way, man! *Iron Man* was really funny, too . . .'

They spent another fifteen minutes discussing the pros and cons of various superhero movies, until Rahul could no longer ignore the half-finished report lying upstairs. Reluctantly, they headed back to the office.

'Hey, so, I don't have any company for the movie,' she said as they neared his desk. 'D'you wanna come with me?'

'Sure,' he said and then belatedly remembered that he had promised Paddy he would watch *Thor* with her. She would throw a fit when he told her he was planning to go with Natasha. Well, he decided, Paddy would just have to deal with it. He had done what she had asked and now Natasha knew he had a girlfriend. There should be no more doubts that she was just a friend, so it was perfectly acceptable for him to go with her.

Reassured by the thought that he was doing nothing wrong, Rahul sat down at his desk with a renewed sense of purpose.

'—never speak to you again, you fucking asshole!' Padmini's angry shout was audible even through the closed bedroom door.

Sameer winced inwardly. So much for having a nice uneventful evening.

It was Friday and they had gone to Aastha's house for Game Night. They'd been halfway through a game of Taboo when Padmini had gotten annoyed by Rahul's continual texting. She'd snapped that he was being rude and asked whom he was messaging.

'Natasha,' Rahul had answered coolly, his eyes hard. 'We're going for *Thor* tomorrow and we were trying to figure out the show timings.'

Padmini had spluttered at him in outrage and then she had stormed into the bedroom, dragging him with her. Not that the closed door was doing a very good job of blocking out what they were saying.

Sameer glanced at Aastha, who was glaring at the door. 'She can't keep letting him treat her like this,' she muttered, more to herself than to Sameer.

Usually, Sameer tried to remain neutral when Paddy and Rahul argued, but this time he had to agree. He had seen some of Natasha's posts on Rahul's wall over the past few weeks. The latest one had been a sentimental poem about friendship which she'd written herself, apparently for him. There was no way *that* could be innocent and he didn't blame Paddy for her reaction.

'He really is being a bit of a jerk,' he said.

Aastha's eyes flickered to his. It was the first time they had been in each other's company since their trip to Goa and there was still a strange tension lingering between them. He noticed, guiltily, that she had dark circles under her eyes.

'You look tired,' he said.

'Just, you know, been busy with work,' she said vaguely.

The evasive reply made him frown.

Rahul's voice rose suddenly, as he shouted the words 'psychotic, possessive bitch' loud enough to wake half the neighbourhood. Sameer's eyes widened. He had witnessed a number of their arguments over the years, but few had been so nasty and vicious.

'God, I am this close to going in there and slapping him,' said Aastha angrily. 'I hope they break up soon. This isn't good for her.'

'I don't know,' he said. 'After so many years, it'll probably be really difficult. Hell, I can't even picture the two of them not dating. They've been "Paddy and Rahul" for so long . . .'

He thought about Karuna then—not that she was ever far from his thoughts these days. He couldn't picture a future in which he wasn't dating her, either, but could he really marry her?

'But that's just . . . like a habit, then,' said Aastha. 'Is that really a reason to stay with someone?'

'Isn't that what marriage is?' he wondered aloud.

She looked surprised. 'Who said anything about marriage?'

He had forgotten whom they were talking about. 'Sorry, I've just had a lot on my mind.'

'Like what?' she asked.

'I talked to Karuna on Monday and she wants to get engaged. She said her parents won't—' He broke off at the sudden stricken look in her eyes. 'Hey, what's wrong?'

'Nothing, just worried about Paddy and Rahul,' she muttered, lowering her gaze. 'What were you saying about Karuna?'

He stared, perplexed by her behaviour. 'I—her parents need a good reason for her to say no to the IIT guy,' he said after a pause. 'She wants to tell them about me—in fact, she has already told her mom. But she says we have to formalize the relationship if there's to be even the tiniest chance of her dad accepting it.'

He waited for Aastha's response, but surprisingly, she didn't say a word.

He hesitated and then continued, 'I don't know, man. I really don't want to break up with her, but getting married? That's too huge. Even if it is after I do my MBA. I'll have to start worrying about getting placed, how much I'm earning . . .' He trailed off.

Aastha was still quiet, her face turned away.

'What, no sage words of advice?' he asked, trying for a light tone and failing. Though he was sometimes irritated by her inability to keep her opinions to herself, he had grown to rely on them, and he wanted to know what she thought about all this.

'It's your decision,' she said in a flat voice. 'It's none of my business.'

'Say what now?' he asked incredulously. 'When the hell did that ever stop you from giving your opinion?'

'I'm not—' she began stiffly, but was interrupted by the bedroom door flying open.

Without looking at either of them, Rahul strode through the living room and walked out of the house, slamming the front door behind him. Aastha was on her feet at once, her face a picture of concern as she hurried to check on Padmini.

Sameer followed her at a slight distance, not sure how welcome he would be. But the bedroom was empty. Instead, from inside the bathroom, he could hear the unmistakable sound of someone throwing up.

'Is everything okay?' he called.

'Can you get a glass of water?' Aastha replied urgently. 'And Polo, too—I saw a pack lying on top of the fridge.'

Sameer did as she asked, cautiously nudging the door when he returned. 'Can I come in?'

'Yeah.'

Paddy was washing her face at the sink. There were tear tracks on her cheeks and her eyes were red-rimmed. Aastha reached for a can of room freshener and sprayed into the air, drowning the lingering smell of vomit. The expression on her face was a mixture of concern for her friend and fury at Rahul.

'Are you falling sick again?' Sameer asked Paddy, handing her the glass of water.

'Not exactly,' Paddy murmured, her cheeks colouring a little. 'This, um, happens sometimes when I fight with Rahul.'

Sameer stared. 'So, you're like, literally lovesick,' he said before he could stop himself.

'Dude,' Aastha hissed at him, but Paddy snorted with laughter, accidentally spraying water everywhere.

'So lame!' She coughed, shaking her head.

He gave her an apologetic look. 'How long has this been going on?' he asked when they had moved from the bathroom to the bedroom.

'A few weeks,' she said with a tinge of self-loathing. 'I know, it's damn pathetic.'

Suddenly, Aastha's overprotective behaviour in Goa made complete sense. His terrible joke notwithstanding, this was really dangerous, depressive kind of behaviour.

'Does Rahul know about this?' he asked.

'No,' she said.

'Shouldn't you tell him?' he asked gently. 'If he could see how much this whole thing is hurting you—'

'Of course he can see,' Padmini said bitterly. 'He's not blind, he just doesn't care.'

'He's actually going for *Thor* with her?' Aastha asked.

'He says I can't have any objection now that she knows he has a girlfriend,' said Paddy. 'I think he resents me for making him tell her and he's trying to get back at me.'

'You shouldn't have had to make him in the first place,' said Aastha angrily. 'You've been dating four years; it's not a fucking secret.'

'He kept saying it never came up,' said Paddy.

'What kind of excuse is that?' Aastha said, even more furious. 'Look, you can't keep letting him do this to you. You know what you should do? Just tell him that if he goes with her for the movie tomorrow, you'll break up with him. And actually follow through on it for once.'

And there was Aastha's pushy well-intentioned advice, given so freely to an unwilling Padmini. *Why had she been so reluctant when he had asked for her opinion*, Sameer wondered.

'I *can't* just break up with him,' Padmini protested.

'It won't really be a break-up,' said Aastha. 'You think he'll survive without you for even a week? He barely lasted two days in Goa.'

'I don't really want to talk about it any more,' said Padmini with a weary air. 'I think I'll just crash, if that's okay.'

'Great idea,' Sameer interjected quickly. Aastha had never been able to understand when it was time to stop pushing. 'Come on,' he said, grabbing her arm without thinking. She went rigid at the contact and he let her go immediately.

Aastha's face was flushed with embarrassment. With downcast eyes, she mumbled a 'good night' to Paddy and left the room quickly. Ignoring the latter's look of confusion, Sameer followed her. He badly wanted to apologize, but Aastha played a song on her phone before he could say anything, raising the volume to drown out any chances of conversation.

It was Saturday night and Padmini was trying to read. Her thoughts were too full of Rahul to allow her to focus and there was little to distract her in the empty house. Usually, she enjoyed having her space and independence, but at times like these, she hated living alone.

The reason she was so miserable was that Rahul had refused to talk to her since their fight. She was going out of her mind with anxiety, even though she knew she was being weak and pathetic. She had told Aastha after Sameer's party that Rahul didn't hold grudges against people, and it was true.

But she had always been the exception to that rule. He was able to go days at a time without talking to her, especially when he thought he was in the right. Padmini couldn't stand the thought of being at odds with him for that long, and she usually gave in and apologized too quickly, even though she knew it only made him take her for granted even more.

She had promised herself not to, but she couldn't stop her traitorous hand from reaching for her phone and dialling his number. He didn't pick up. Panic and fury rose in her gut. Had he really gone for the movie with Natasha?

She screwed her eyes shut and dialled Karuna's number, desperate to talk to someone about this.

'Hey, what's up?'

'I hate him,' she said.

'Who, Rahul?' she asked.

'Who else?'

'What'd he do now?'

Padmini poured out the entire story. 'He says she doesn't have too many friends besides him, because she lost touch with all of them while she was dating her ex. Which, I'm sorry, just shows that she's really pathetic, but of course he doesn't see that. He thinks she's all lonely and heartbroken and needs a shoulder to cry on. It's complete bullshit! How does he not see that it's really screwed up that he's her *only* friend? They only met, what, a few months ago?'

'He's being a complete jerk,' said Karuna.

'I know,' Paddy agreed wearily. 'I don't know what to do. If he goes for the movie, what's the next step? Dinner? Staying over at her house—oh, but wait, he's already done that. Aastha says I should try to stop talking to him for a week, but it's too hard. As it is, I keep throwing up all the time—'

'Wait, what?' Karuna interrupted. 'Don't tell me you're having another pregnancy scare.'

'No, nothing like that,' she said. 'I—it happens sometimes when I fight with him.'

'That's not good,' said Karuna, after a shocked pause.

'I know, but I don't know what to do about it,' said Padmini. 'And I can't figure out what to do about Rahul, either. Do you think I should break up with him?'

'I don't know,' came the slow thoughtful reply. 'You've been dating—how long has it been, three years?'

'Four,' said Karuna.

'Oh, yeah. That's not an easy thing to give up. And he did tell Natasha you're his girlfriend, didn't he?'

'He *says* he did,' said Paddy darkly. 'I don't really know for sure, do I?'

'You seriously think he'd lie about that?' Karuna asked.

'No,' said Padmini reluctantly. 'I'm just being paranoid.'

'I don't think you should break up with him yet,' said Karuna. 'But I do think you should get the message across to him that you just *won't* accept it if he goes out with her alone like this. You need to show him you're serious about that.'

Padmini wondered how exactly she was supposed to do that—she'd yelled, cried, threatened to break up with Rahul and even come close to slapping him, but nothing seemed to make an impression. Feeling disheartened, she mumbled something about work and hung up.

———

Rahul stared at his phone. There were two messages and three missed calls from Paddy, and that was only since that morning. He hadn't taken her calls the whole of yesterday and he knew she was probably going out of her mind with anxiety. His anger had abated a while ago, and he wanted more than anything to talk to her and smooth things over.

But the prospect of having to justify his going for the movie with Natasha, of Padmini crying and threatening to break up with him, and then calling him back within two hours deterred him—it had all become so boringly predictable and unpleasant. In his heart, though, he knew that the longer he waited to call her, the worse the ensuing conversation would be, so he steeled himself and dialled her number. She picked up on the first ring. 'Hey.'

'Hey,' he said and waited for the inevitable.

'Did you go for *Thor* with her?'

'Yeah,' he said. 'It was a great movie.'

'I'm sure it was,' she said bitterly.

'It's not like anything happened. How many times do I have to tell you that we're just friends?'

'You know what I don't get?' she said as if she hadn't heard him. 'We've dated four years and you're still willing to make me completely miserable for a girl you met months ago. How can you possibly say you don't have a thing for her?'

'God, why are you always so tedious?' he snapped, irritated. 'It's always the same damn thing. Can't we talk about something other than Natasha for two seconds? Oh, I'm sorry, I forgot, this is where you threaten to break up with me again.'

'You're being really mean,' she said, her tears welling up again.

He forced himself to take a deep breath. 'I went for a movie with a friend. I'm not going to apologize for it. How's your weekend been?'

There was a long silence and then she replied in a thin exhausted voice, 'Fine. Watched TV and read.'

'No manuscripts to edit?' He cringed even as he asked

the question, because it was so obviously an attempt to make conversation.

'No,' said Paddy.

'That's good.'

There was another long silence.

He cast about for something to say, but drew a blank. Suddenly, he felt immeasurably tired—it shouldn't be this much of an effort to have a conversation with his girlfriend. 'Listen, I think I'll hang up. I kind of want an afternoon nap after lunch.'

'Sure,' she said.

'Maybe I'll come over a little later,' he said, not really meaning it.

'Yeah,' she said. 'Bye, then.'

She hung up. He felt a twinge of something like guilt, but dismissed it immediately. He had done nothing to be ashamed of.

SIXTEEN

Karuna knew she needed to concentrate. Her exams were two weeks away and she needed to do at least ten mock tests before that. But try as she might, her mind refused to cooperate. She kept thinking about Sameer, wondering what decision he would make, and what she would do if he said he wasn't ready to get married.

Her mother's increasing suspicion of her weighed on her, too. She was full of questions whenever Karuna went out, even if it was just for her coaching classes.

Her phone rang and her heart sank when she saw Joseph's name flashing on the screen. He'd been calling her frequently over the past weeks. She slid her thumb across her phone screen and pressed it to her ear. 'Hello?'

'So guess what? I went to a proper comic-book convention.'

Despite herself, she smiled at his enthusiasm. 'How was it?'

'It was awesome!' he said. 'People came dressed as Batman and Superman, and there were even a couple of women in slutty Wonder Woman costumes.'

'Seriously?' She laughed. 'Sounds like something straight out of a *Big Bang Theory* episode.'

'Yeah,' he said. 'So how's everything at your end?'

She hesitated. Suddenly, she wanted nothing more than to just come clean with him about everything, to tell him about Sameer and the rest of it. But she stopped herself as she always did, because she still didn't know him well enough to trust him with that.

'Fine,' she said. 'Busy studying for my next exam.'

'How many have you cleared?' he asked.

'This will be my sixth,' she said.

'Really?' He sounded surprised. 'I thought they took years—didn't you just finish your postgrad?'

'Almost a year ago, actually,' she said. 'And I did the first couple of exams while doing my MSc. But the later ones are a lot tougher. I've never been that great at multitasking, so I thought I'd take some time off, go for coaching and clear as many as I could. I know most people do it while working, but it takes twice as long.'

'Sounds scary,' said Joseph.

The conversation moved easily to other topics. Even though she dreaded his phone calls, Joseph was a very easy person to talk to and they had a lot in common. When she happened to glance at her watch some time later, she realized with a start that half an hour had passed before she had even registered it. She hung up quickly, telling him that she needed to study. His voice was warm when he wished her goodbye.

She sat on her bed, heart beating a little too fast as she realized how far she had let things go with Joseph. What if Sameer decided he wanted to marry her and she broke it off with Joseph without any warning? He didn't deserve to be hurt like that.

Almost before she had decided to do it, she was dialling Sameer's number.

He picked up on the fifth ring. 'Hey, you.'

'Busy?' she asked.

'No, just watching a show,' he said. 'What's up?'

She took a deep breath and confessed, 'I'm kind of freaking out,' she said. 'Joseph is calling me more and more often and I think he's getting too attached to me. He's due back in less than a month and he'll want to meet me when he gets here.'

'You have to say no,' said Sameer sharply. 'That's just—'

'I know that,' she interrupted forcefully. 'But I told you, I can't just say no if I don't have a good excuse. Have you thought about the whole marriage thing?'

'It's been a week since we had that conversation,' he said, an edge to his voice. 'You really expect me to make up my mind that quickly?'

'No, of course not,' she said. 'I just need to know you're thinking about it! You never even mention it when we talk; I don't even *know* if you're taking this seriously—'

'Are you kidding me?' he interrupted. 'How could I not be thinking about it all the time? I mean, you proposed to me completely out of the blue, even though you know I have no plans of getting married—'

'That's bullshit!' she retorted. 'You've always known what kind of family I come from. If you wanted a future with me, this was always going to come up. How the fuck was I supposed to know you didn't have plans to get married until after you turn thirty?'

'I think it's completely unfair of you to put this all on me,' he snapped. 'You could just say no to Joseph and live with the consequences, but you won't even bloody consider doing that! And you expect me to change my entire life around for you?'

Karuna sucked in her breath. He was being completely insensitive. 'You aren't being fair,' she said. 'I need to know where *we* stand before I tell my parents anything. That's not an unreasonable thing for me to ask.'

'Maybe it isn't,' he conceded grudgingly. 'But you need to understand that I can't just make a decision like this overnight, either.'

'Can you at least tell me in a month?' she pleaded. 'That's when Joseph gets back from the US.'

'And what if I say no?' he asked sharply. 'Will you actually marry him?'

The thought made her shudder. 'I don't want to think about that. And in any case, this is about you and me, not him. I just need to know.'

'I don't like the fact that you're giving me a deadline,' Sameer said. 'That isn't right.'

'Well, I don't like it either, but I can't really help it, can I?' she snapped, and then closed her eyes and pinched the bridge of her nose. Yelling at him wasn't going to help matters. 'Sorry.'

He sighed and she could sense his anger dissipating, too. 'I promise I'll think about it,' he said in a calmer tone. 'But you need to promise me you won't keep bringing it up, or putting pressure on me. This has to be my decision.'

'I guess that's fair,' she said grudgingly.

There was a long pause. 'I should get back to studying, then,' she said.

'Yeah,' he said. 'I'll talk to you in a day or two.'

'I love you,' she said suddenly, a little desperately.

'I love you, too,' he said. 'Bye.'

He hung up, leaving her staring blankly at the wall of her bedroom.

———

'Karuna? Can I talk to you for a minute?'

Surprised, Karuna looked up from her textbook. Her father was standing at the door, a grim expression on his face.

She sat up. 'What is it?'

He didn't reply, but instead glanced around the room disapprovingly. 'Why don't you ever sit at your desk? We spent good money on it and you sprawl on your bed as if you don't have anywhere else to study. You'll ruin your back like this.'

Sometimes, it really felt as if her father hadn't noticed she wasn't in school any more. 'I study better when I'm lying down.'

He waved this away impatiently and sat down next to her. 'I wanted to talk to you about Joseph.'

Her wariness increased. 'What about him?'

'Your mother says you've been talking to him regularly.'

'Not like I have any choice in the matter,' she said.

He sighed in exasperation. 'Must you be so difficult? I wanted to ask what you think of him now that you're getting to know him better.'

'I don't want to marry him,' she said stubbornly.

'That isn't what I asked you,' he said.

'He's a little boring,' she lied.

He looked disappointed and annoyed. 'I wish you could just be honest,' he said. 'I've heard you on the phone with him when I walked past your room; it's obvious you don't hate him.'

Karuna was completely fed up with her father's hypocrisy. 'Why are you even pretending you care whether I like him or not, Appa?' she asked. 'It doesn't make any difference to you what I want. Even if I hated him, you'd find a way to make us keep talking to each other, because you're so convinced you're right about this.'

Her father looked disgusted. 'I don't know why I bother,' he said. 'It's as if the only thing that matters to you is that *we* chose this boy for you and, therefore, there *has* to be something wrong with him.'

Considering all the compromises she had already made for her parents' sake, this struck Karuna as very unjust. 'I could say the exact same thing,' she retorted, wounded. 'Just because you think I'm being stubborn and immature, you disregard everything I say. What will it take to convince you this isn't right for me?'

'And what will it take for you to give him a fair chance and see if he could make you happy?' her father countered as if he hadn't heard a word of what she had just said.

'I think you just want me to say I like him so you can feel less guilty about forcing me into this,' she said viciously.

She knew from the look on his face that she had hurt him. She couldn't bring herself to care. 'I don't feel guilty about anything,' he said in a tight voice. 'I think you should feel ashamed of how you are treating us, when we're doing this for your future.'

He walked out of the room and Karuna found herself blinking back tears. She would have thought she'd have gotten used to these conversations by now, but it still broke her heart every time she argued with her parents. There had been a time when she could do no wrong in their eyes and she hated being forced into this role.

Not for the first time, she wondered how all this would end. She wished she could just skip ahead a couple of years to see what her life would look like. Right now, everything seemed completely uncertain and she didn't know how she was going to survive the next few weeks.

SEVENTEEN

Aastha lay on the beanbag in her living room, watching the whirring ceiling fan. She had a set of proofs lying in her bag, waiting to be edited, but she didn't have the energy to do any work.

Ever since she had found out that Sameer was thinking about marrying Karuna, she'd had no peace of mind. The thought of him being so completely out of her reach—not that she harboured much hope of his returning her feelings as things stood right now—was surprisingly painful.

It was only a few weeks ago that they'd had a purely platonic relationship. Had that one night really had such a profound impact on her? She'd searched her mind and realized that it wasn't just the physical attraction. He was also her best friend and one of the kindest people she knew. She knew, instinctively, that no one would ever be able to understand her better than him and that was what she had become so drawn to.

It crushed her when he talked to her about Karuna. Though he tried to be offhand and casual when he mentioned her, she could tell he was struggling, and desperately wanted her opinion. If this had happened before Goa, Aastha wouldn't have hesitated to tell him what she thought. She would have told him not to compromise on his career when he was so young and that he needed to figure out what he wanted from life before he settled down. But now, with her ever-present feelings for him, she was afraid she was being biased.

'What are you doing?'

She started. Nainika, her flatmate, was standing above her, looking at her quizzically. 'When did you get back?' she asked.

'Ten minutes ago!' Nainika replied, surprised. 'Didn't you hear me unlock the door?'

'No,' said Aastha, embarrassed. 'I guess I spaced out.'

Nainika sat down on the sofa, looking concerned. 'Why are you just lying here like this? Is everything okay?'

'Not really,' said Aastha.

'What happened?'

Aastha knew that Nainika was the one person she could talk to about this, because they didn't have any friends in common. But it still wasn't easy to put into words. 'Just some shit with Sameer,' she said finally.

'Did you guys have a fight?'

'Worse,' said Aastha. She gave her a wan smile. 'I figured out I have feelings for him.'

Nainika's eyebrows shot up. 'Okay . . . how did that happen?'

'Does it really matter?' Aastha asked, not wanting to go into the details. 'I don't know what to do. Everything's become so weird between us lately—'

'Wait, you told him you have feelings for him?' Nainika interrupted.

'No, but I think he's guessed,' said Aastha. 'I'm not a very good actress.' She sighed and added, 'He's thinking of getting married to Karuna.'

'Wow,' said Nainika. 'That really sucks.'

'Tell me about it,' said Aastha. 'The worst part is, he keeps asking me for advice. He's unsure if he should marry her, but I really don't know what I'm supposed to say! It's not like I can be very objective about it.'

'He keeps asking you even though he knows you have feelings for him?' Nainika asked, frowning. 'He's never struck me as insensitive.'

'He's not,' said Aastha immediately. 'He just—I'm his closest friend, right? I was the person he always talked to about Karuna before all this happened. This is a huge decision and he wants to know my opinion. I don't think he knows how serious my crush is, or he wouldn't keep asking.' She realized that she'd given away more than she had intended.

Nainika, of course, picked up on it immediately. 'How serious?' she asked. 'Would you date him if he wasn't with Karuna?'

'In a heartbeat,' she answered, without even needing to think about it.

'Wow,' said Nainika. 'I really don't know what to say.'

'There's nothing *to* say,' said Aastha. 'Leave it, it doesn't matter.'

'Well, I know this doesn't fix anything, but Avinash and I are going out with a few friends,' said Nainika. 'Do you want to join us? It might take your mind off things.'

'It's a weeknight,' said Aastha.

'So? You're not in school.'

That was true. 'Where are you guys going?' she asked.

'Route 69,' said Nainika. 'It's an open-air pub. Good food, alcohol, but no loud music or dancing. And it won't be crowded.'

Aastha considered it and nodded. 'That actually sounds pretty good,' she said.

'You should get ready then; we're leaving in half an hour.'

She ended up enjoying it more than she had expected. This was the first time Aastha had ever gone out with Nainika's friends. It was nice to be surrounded by relative strangers for a few hours and the food had been excellent. All in all, it was a welcome distraction from thinking about Sameer all the time.

The next evening, Sameer sent her a text asking if she was free to meet for dinner. Her stomach flip-flopped. For only a moment, she was very tempted to make an excuse and beg off, but told herself she was being ridiculous. This was *Sameer* and, no matter how awkward things might seem, she refused to believe they had reached the point where she had to think twice about spending time with him. She said yes and they decided on a restaurant in Ambience Mall.

Aastha got there first, but it wasn't long before Sameer walked in, too. Since he had come directly from work, he was dressed in a formal shirt and trousers. Her heart skipped a beat at how handsome he looked. She scowled, angry with herself for being such a typical girl, and his smile changed to a questioning look.

'What's wrong?'

'Nothing,' she said. 'How's it going?'

'Not great,' said Sameer.

She could sense that he was about to mention Karuna, so she quickly interjected, 'I'm starving, can we order?'

He looked a little startled by her abruptness, but obliged her by opening the menu card and giving it a cursory glance. She studied him surreptitiously as she glanced over her own. He looked tired, as if he hadn't been sleeping very well.

'So how's work?' she asked when they had placed their order.

'Fine,' he said. 'Nothing new. You?'

'Oh, you know, just editing, proofing . . . the same old thing,' she said. 'It's boring, but I try not to let it get to me too much.'

He nodded and fell silent. Aastha didn't blame him—she couldn't believe things had become so awkward between them that they had to resort to this sort of empty small talk. She tried to think of something genuine to say that would get the conversation going, but he beat her to it.

'I've been thinking a lot lately. About Karuna, I mean. I don't know what to do and it's driving me insane. If I do . . . marry her, my whole life will change completely. I can't even imagine that kind of responsibility. And if I don't marry her . . . I can't imagine that either.'

Aastha stared at the table, torn. She wanted to tell him that if he was this unsure, he probably wasn't ready for such a serious commitment. But she didn't know if she really believed that, or if it was because she couldn't stand the thought of him getting married.

'Do you really have nothing to say about this?' Sameer asked as the silence stretched. 'You, of all people?'

'It's not my place to say anything,' said Aastha, her voice tight.

'Why do you keep saying that?' said Sameer, frustrated. 'I hate this. I know what happened in Goa was awful, but—?'

'Can we not talk about that?'

'We have to!' he exclaimed. 'Things have become way too tense and awkward between us, and I know that's my fault. You need to let me apologize and then we have to talk it through, or we'll never—'

'Sameer, I *cannot* talk about this,' she interrupted shakily. 'Please.'

He stared at her, shocked by the depth of her reaction. 'Aastha . . .' he began helplessly and then stopped. He obviously had no idea what to say to her.

Aastha rose abruptly, muttering something about having to pee, and headed for the nearest bathroom. She was furious with herself. She couldn't believe she had cried in front of him, *again*. He was probably convinced she was madly in love with him after this and she herself was beginning to wonder if she was.

Her phone buzzed incessantly in her jeans pocket and she knew without having to check that Sameer was trying to call her. She made an effort to compose herself and headed back to him.

'I'm sorry,' he said when he saw her. 'I shouldn't have brought it up when I know you're not comfortable talking about it. I won't talk about it again, I promise.'

She swallowed hard at the finality in his words. 'I'm sorry, too,' she said. 'I don't mean to be this pathetic—'

'No,' he said fiercely. 'You don't get to feel bad about this, okay? This is *not* your fault, at all.' Changing the subject deliberately, he asked, 'So, anything new at work?'

'You already asked me that,' she reminded him softly.

'Oh, yeah,' he said.

Silence fell again. They both cast about for things to say,

but every attempt they made stuttered to an awkward halt. It was with relief that they parted ways later and Aastha knew that Sameer wouldn't ask to meet her alone again after this.

EIGHTEEN

Resounding music, whiffs of cigarette smoke and the half-drunken laughter of colleagues washed over Rahul's senses. He rolled his shoulders, trying to shake off a week's worth of tension.

It had been a busy period at work. Now, they had completed their project and the three teams that had worked on it had decided to celebrate by going out for drinks. Rahul had originally planned to go to Paddy's house in the evening, but the prospect of going back to her, when she'd been so dull and distant lately, had not been very appealing.

He had called her and told her he was coming late, expecting her to get angry, but she had only asked once if Natasha would be there too, and then gone very quiet when he said she would. Though he'd been slightly confused by the lack of reaction, he'd been too relieved to probe any further.

Taking a swig of beer, he stared across the table at Natasha. She was looking radiant in a low-necked, clingy black dress which showed off her curvy figure to advantage.

'What?' she shouted over the music, noticing his stare.

'Nothing,' he said. 'You look really nice today.'

'Thanks,' she said, beaming at him.

The woman sitting next to him rose to join the crowd on the dance floor, and Natasha got up and slid into the empty space. Her dress rode up a little as she sat down and he didn't quite succeed in his valiant attempt not to look at her bare thighs.

'This place has great music, doesn't it?' she said.

'Yeah,' he said, reaching for the plate of French fries in front of him and popping a few of them into his mouth.

'I swear this is just what I needed after the week I've had,' she said, leaning close to him and speaking into his ear. 'My boss has been on my case 24/7 and then Abhi kept missed-calling me all week.'

'He did?' Rahul asked, feeling a twinge of something he refused to define. 'Why?'

'God knows,' said Natasha. 'I didn't take his calls; I'm done taking shit from him. I just want to have a good time tonight and forget about everything else.'

Rahul could completely relate to that. He smiled at her and took another swig of beer. It was his third and there was now a pleasant buzz running through his limbs.

'Oh, I love this song,' Natasha said as the music changed. 'Do you wanna dance?'

'Sure, why not?' he said, getting up.

Grabbing his beer, he followed her on to the dance floor. They joined a group of their colleagues, all in varying stages of drunkenness as they moved to the music. Rahul bobbed his head, enjoying the pounding beat from the speakers near him. He couldn't remember the last time he'd had so much fun.

The night passed in a haze of alcohol and cigarette smoke. Natasha stayed beside him for most of the night, but some of her colleagues dragged her away at some point. When it was nearing midnight and the music started grating on Rahul's ears, he slipped outside. The pub had a small open-air compound outside, with a few cushioned chairs and tables where people could sit.

Rahul made his way to one of them, lurching as he walked. The air outside was comfortingly cool after the crowd inside and he sank down into a sofa. He inhaled deeply and closed his eyes, enjoying the breeze.

Natasha's voice startled him out of his daze. 'Hey, you disappeared on me.'

He opened his eyes and smiled lazily. 'It was too loud in there.'

She sat down beside him. The sofa was narrow, so they ended up pressed together. He stared down at his jeans-clad knee beside her milky white skin and felt his mouth go suddenly dry. He forced his gaze up to hers.

'You know, I had no idea you could dance for so long,' Natasha said softly. 'Impressive stamina.'

'Only when I'm drunk,' he said with a muted chuckle. 'And anyway, I could say the same about you.'

'I'm pretty drunk too,' she confessed with a grin.

'What time is it?' he asked.

She glanced at her watch. 'Quarter to twelve. The bar will be closing soon; I'd better call a cab.'

'You're going home alone?' he asked, concerned.

'It's a Meru,' she said.

'At this hour, nothing is safe. I'll drop you.'

'Thank you.'

Silence again. She leaned her head against his shoulder

and murmured, 'I'm tired.'

He glanced down at her and something fluttered in his chest.

'I'm too comfortable to move,' she said, snuggling closer to him and turning her face upwards. 'I wish we could stay here all night.'

They were silent for a few minutes, staring at each other, and then she leaned up and pressed her lips to his. Something, a warning, twinged in his chest, but it was too muted to drown out the softness of her mouth against his. Before he knew it, his lips were moving in tandem with hers, the fruity taste of flavoured lip gloss spreading over his senses. The kiss deepened. Instinctively, he darted his tongue out gently against hers. She moaned.

The soft sensual sound was enough to shock him back to reality. He pulled away from her violently, his heart pounding. *What had he just done?*

'Rahul?' she asked, confused.

His hand rose involuntarily to wipe his mouth. 'I have a girlfriend,' he said in a hollow voice.

Natasha shifted away from him, her face colouring. 'It's just a bit of fun,' she said. 'I'm in no shape for anything serious either, after Abhi, so I thought—'

'I've been dating her for five years,' he blurted out.

She stared at him in shock, which quickly turned to anger. She got up and stood in front of him, hands on her hips. 'You never told me that,' she said. 'Were you just leading me on, all this time?'

'Don't you dare act all innocent,' he fired back. 'You kissed me first and you *knew* I had a girlfriend, so don't you fucking *dare* act like this is all my fault.'

She reeled back, her eyes filling with tears. Turning abruptly, she made her way back into the club. Rahul made no move to stop her.

He couldn't believe he had kissed her. He had been so sure that there had been nothing between them but friendship, so completely, arrogantly sure that he would never cheat on Paddy. He had called her possessive, psychotic, jealous—and all along, she'd been *right*. He hated her a little for that, but he hated himself more. For a while, he was so wracked by shame and guilt that he couldn't think.

Then his mind turned back to Paddy and he thought about how he should handle this. His first instinct was to keep this from her and pretend as if nothing had happened. Wouldn't it only hurt her if he told her the truth? But he knew it was a hollow justification and, besides, he didn't know if he could live with that kind of guilt hanging over him. Paddy knew him too well not to notice immediately that something was up. But if he told her . . .

After the Purnima episode she had told him that if he ever cheated on her, they'd be finished for good. What if she ever found out about this later, from a stray text message or office gossip? She would never believe him then and they really would be finished. He knew, no matter how hard it would be, he would have to tell her the truth.

The prospect filled him with dread and, suddenly, all he wanted was to drive to her house and get it off his chest. But it wouldn't be fair to wake her up and blurt this out in the middle of the night. If he told her in the morning, at least she would be able to call Aastha over for moral support.

He cringed at the thought of what Aastha would have to say about this. He had just confirmed every bad thing she had ever said or thought about him. He realized that if Padmini did break up with him, he would lose all his friends. Aastha would obviously be on Paddy's side in all this, and Sameer was too close to Aastha to risk upsetting her by talking to him.

The worst part was, he wouldn't be able to blame any of them.

Padmini woke up on Saturday morning with a clawing sensation in her chest. Sunlight streamed in through her bedroom window, but that wasn't what had woken her. There was a nagging feeling she couldn't shake off, as if something was very wrong. Before she knew it, she was dialling Rahul's number.

To her surprise, he picked up on the first ring. 'Hey,' he said, sounding tired.

'Hey, how come you're up so early?'

'I don't know, just happened to be awake, I guess.'

Her sense of foreboding increased. 'I thought you would have been up late last night, with the party and all,' she said.

He didn't say anything for a long moment and then asked abruptly, 'Listen, can I come over? Like, now?'

'Uh, sure,' she said, surprised but not displeased. 'You want breakfast? I could make you some eggs—'

'Don't bother,' he interrupted her. 'I'll be over in a few minutes.'

'Sure,' she said, throwing off her covers and getting out of bed. She was about to hang up when he said softly, 'Paddy?'

'Yeah?' she said.

'I love you,' he said. 'You know that, right?'

'Of course I do,' she said. 'Wha—why are you being so senti all of a sudden?'

'Never mind,' he said. 'See you in a few minutes.'

———————

Rahul's heart was in his mouth as he climbed the stairs leading up to Padmini's apartment. He tried to rehearse telling her about the kiss, to plan what he would say, but try as he might, the words wouldn't come to him.

When he reached her door, he stood there for a long moment, still and silent. A thought struck him and he sent a quick text to Aastha before he turned off his phone. Screwing up his courage, he rang the doorbell.

Paddy opened it almost immediately, a too-bright smile on her face. 'Hey,' she said with a cheeriness that he could tell wasn't genuine. 'I made you scrambled eggs.'

'You did?' he said, his insides twisting with guilt. 'I told you not to bother.'

'I was making them for myself anyway, it was no trouble,' she said.

He followed her into the kitchen, watching as she served the scrambled eggs on two plates. She was wearing one of his office shirts and a pair of tattered pyjamas, but he still thought she looked beautiful. With a renewed pang, he realized he couldn't think of the last time he had stopped to notice that.

'D'you want toast?' she asked.

'No thanks.'

She handed him a plate and they both went to the tiny living room and sat down on the sofa. 'How was the party?' Paddy asked, her voice still sounding forced.

'Can we finish eating first before we talk?'

'Sure,' she said.

He forced himself to swallow the scrambled eggs she had made for him, even though his appetite had completely vanished. Paddy took a long time too, picking at her food and taking tiny bites. When they were both finished, Rahul said, 'I have to tell you something.'

'About the party?' she asked. There was an expression of dread on her face.

He nodded tersely, unable to meet her eyes. There was a long heavy silence. 'Natasha kissed me.'

'What?'

'And I kissed her back,' he finished.

He waited for her anger, but it never came. Instead, she made a strangled noise, clamped her hand to her mouth and rushed into the bathroom. He leapt to his feet and followed her, and was horrified to find her throwing up everything that she had just eaten.

He reached towards her to rub her back, but she recoiled from him. There were tears streaming down her face.

'I'm so sorry,' he said. 'I was drunk, and I just . . . I don't know what happened to me. I stopped it before I went very far, I swear—'

'Shut up,' she said hoarsely, her eyes bloodshot.

He bowed his head and waited until she finished. A few minutes later, she flushed the toilet and rose shakily, leaning against the sink. He waited for her to say something, to scream and curse, but she didn't say a word, just stared at him tiredly with her eyes dripping and her cheeks all blotchy.

'Please say something,' he said when he couldn't take the silence any more.

'There's nothing to say,' she said. 'I'm done with you.'

He said desperately, 'I know you're shocked, I know I betrayed you—'

She let out a broken laugh and said, 'I'm not shocked.'

He flinched. 'What?'

'After you went for that movie with her, I knew this was going to happen. It's sort of a relief that it's not hanging over my head any more.'

Her resigned, exhausted tone cut him to the quick and his eyes filled. 'Why aren't you yelling at me?' he whispered. 'You should be furious. This is the worst thing I've ever done.'

'Honestly, I don't have the energy,' she said. 'You need to leave, right now. And don't try to call me. We're over.'

The finality in the words made wetness slide over his cheeks. 'Paddy, please. I know I made a mistake, but please don't throw away five years because of that. I'm begging you.'

'No one has ever hurt me worse than you,' she said, closing her eyes tightly. 'I can't let you do that to me any more.'

The words hurt far worse than if she had yelled or screamed or even slapped him. He turned woodenly and left her standing there, crying.

There was nothing he could do.

NINETEEN

Aastha's breath came in quick pants as she hurried up the two flights of stairs leading to Padmini's apartment. She had been panicking for the entire length of her journey from Gurgaon, and had all but run to Paddy's house from the Malviya Nagar metro station. Though she had been calling her friend's phone non-stop since she had received Rahul's text message, there had been no response.

She charged around the corner leading to her friend's apartment and nearly crashed into Rahul. Her alarm increased when she saw that his face was streaked with tears.

'What the hell happened?' she demanded.

He shook his head and continued down the stairs without replying.

Frantic, she rang Padmini's doorbell. There was no response. She cursed and kept ringing, until suddenly the door flew open to reveal a furious Padmini. 'Rahul, can't you just *fuck off*—' She broke off in surprise. 'Aastha?'

'I got a text from Rahul telling me to come over right now because you needed me. What the hell happened?'

Padmini's face crumpled and she burst into sobs. 'He kissed her,' she said.

'What?'

'Natasha—God, I feel so sick—I can't even, I don't—'

'Okay, hey, you need to breathe,' said Aastha, steering her hyperventilating friend back into the apartment and towards the sofa.

Padmini slumped down on it and Aastha sat next to her, wrapping an arm around her shaking shoulders. 'What happened, exactly?'

She sniffed loudly and when she spoke her words were choppy. 'He—there was an office party last night and he was drunk. She kissed him and he didn't stop it. He kissed her back.'

'Bastard!' Aastha spat out, furious. 'Please tell me you broke up with him?'

'Yeah, of course,' said Paddy tiredly. 'I'm done with him. Just thinking about him makes me feel sick to my stomach.'

'You threw up again?' Aastha asked with concern.

'I made him eggs for breakfast. Pathetic, right? Here he cheated on me and I'm making him breakfast . . .' She gave a disgusted laugh. 'Obviously, I threw up the second he told me.'

'You need to eat something,' said Aastha. 'What else is in the kitchen? Cereal?'

Padmini shook her head. 'I'm really not hungry. I'll probably throw up everything I eat today, anyway.'

Aastha had been afraid of that. 'You're going to be okay,' she told her friend. 'This seems like the worst thing ever right now, but in a year, you'll look back on this without feeling awful.'

This didn't seem to have much of an impact. Instead, Padmini continued as if she hadn't heard her. 'Do you know what's strange? I sort of knew. I had a feeling that something was wrong and he proved me right.'

'You're better off,' said Aastha firmly. 'I always thought you deserved a lot better.'

Paddy grimaced. 'I don't really need to hear that now,' she said.

'Sorry.' Aastha changed the subject. 'Let's watch *Big Bang Theory*. And order chocolate ice cream—that makes everything better.'

Paddy gave her a weak smile. 'Yes to the *Big Bang Theory*, but no to the ice cream. I *really* don't feel like eating.'

She stared at her friend, worried. She resolved to keep a close eye on Paddy over the next few weeks.

They spent the rest of the morning in bed, watching their favourite episodes. However, Paddy was in her own world for most of that time and barely responded even in the funniest moments. Rahul tried to call her once around noon and she cut the call immediately before dissolving into tears once again.

Aastha grabbed the phone from her hand and switched it off. Padmini didn't protest.

A few minutes later, she received a text from Rahul on her phone.

How is she?

Her response was instant and furious. *Fuck off.*

There was, thankfully, no response. Aastha couldn't believe he had the gall to ask about Paddy in the first place, after what he'd done. She was irrationally annoyed with Padmini, too, for not being angrier with Rahul. She wanted her to call Rahul and scream at him, not keep moping around and crying. But she kept this to herself, knowing it was hurtful and unfair.

More than anything, Aastha wanted to call Sameer and tell him what had happened. She was worried about Paddy and was afraid that she'd fall sick if she kept refusing to eat. But the memory of their awkward meeting the previous night was still too fresh in her mind.

————

As he walked away from Padmini's house, Rahul felt disconnected from everything around him. The guilt sweeping through him was so powerful that it drowned out everything else and, for a while, he just drove aimlessly through the lanes around Padmini's building, wondering what to do with himself.

Every time he passed her house, his gaze would flick upwards involuntarily and he would picture again the devastated look in her eyes. He grew so wretched that he even tried to call her, even though he knew he should leave her alone. She hung up without speaking to him and when he tried to ask Aastha about her, he got an angry message in response.

He swallowed his pride. After all, he had been the one to call Aastha in the first place and she had every right to treat him like this. He was sure she had told Sameer by now, too. None of them would ever forgive him for this.

Sighing, he headed back home. He would have spent the rest of the day moping around, but he had another project deadline coming up the following week, so he was busy for the rest of the day. It was nearing eight when Sameer's name flashed on his phone.

'Hello?' he asked tentatively.

'Hey, Rahul,' said Sameer, casual and friendly as ever. 'I was wondering if you were free tonight. I just read a review of *Pacific Rim*; it's supposed to be great . . . and there's a 9.30 show in PVR Saket.'

Rahul blinked in surprise. 'I, uh . . .'

'Dude, don't tell me you and Paddy are still fighting,' said Sameer. 'Just get over yourself and apologize already.'

There was a startled pause.

'Sameer, didn't Aastha tell you?' Rahul asked after a few moments.

'Tell me what?'

Rahul took a deep breath. 'Paddy and I broke up this morning.'

'*What*? What the hell?'

'I really don't want to talk about it,' said Rahul. 'Why don't you just ask Aastha? I'm sure she'd be more than happy to fill you in,' he said bitterly.

'I'm asking you,' Sameer persisted.

'I kissed Natasha,' Rahul said after a long pause. 'Last night, at the office party.'

'You did what?' Sameer exclaimed. 'What the fuck is wrong with you?'

'I know,' said Rahul shakily. 'I guess you're going to hang up on me now?'

'Yeah, because I can't talk on the phone while I drive,' said Sameer. 'I'm coming over to see you.'

'Huh?'

'You sound like you're this close to jumping off the nearest building,' said Sameer.

'But . . . I'm the asshole in all this,' Rahul whispered, his mind reeling.

'And what, I'm supposed to stop talking to you forever because you made a stupid mistake?' Sameer asked, exasperated.

That's what Aastha would do, Rahul thought, but he didn't say it aloud for fear of offending Sameer. 'I guess not,' he said, still stunned.

'Then I'll see you in a bit,' said Sameer, and hung up.

Rahul stared at the phone, wondering if he had imagined the entire conversation.

——————

'You and Paddy will work things out,' Sameer told Rahul for what felt like the hundredth time. 'Yeah, you messed up, but I honestly don't see you breaking up for good over this.' *They were far too dependent on each other for that*, Sameer thought, though he didn't say that aloud.

'I don't know,' said Rahul, scrubbing at his face anxiously. 'She was really upset. She threw up when I told her.'

'Again?' said Sameer, frowning in concern. 'That's not good.'

'What d'you mean, again?' Rahul asked.

Sameer faltered, surprised. 'It's . . . she gets sick sometimes, when you guys are figh—I mean, when she gets upset. Didn't you know that?'

'No,' Rahul said, horrified. 'I had no idea! I actually made her physically sick? Why didn't she tell me she was that upset? I would have stopped meeting Natasha. I *would have*.'

'Hey, calm down,' said Sameer, alarmed. 'I know that. So will she if you apologize to her enough times.'

But Rahul's expression remained angry and pained. 'I can't believe how much I've hurt her,' he said, more to himself than to Sameer. 'I was so sure that there was nothing between me and Natasha, so sure I could never *really* cheat on her. How could I have been so fucking blind?'

Sameer watched him, unable to think of anything he could say to make him feel better. He *had* been awful to Paddy and now he would have to deal with the consequences. Sameer was sure that Rahul wouldn't lose Paddy for good, that they would manage to work things out, but he also wondered if she would ever be able to trust him completely after this.

Finally, he did the only thing he could think of to help, and pulled out the beers he had stopped to buy on his way there. His friend accepted one with a grateful nod and they sat together in Rahul's living room, swigging at their beers in silence.

After a while, Rahul said quietly, 'Thank you for coming today, Sameer. I can't believe you drove all the way here from Gurgaon just to check if I was okay. For that matter, I can't believe you're still talking to me.'

Sameer stared at him in surprise. 'Why wouldn't I be talking to you?' he asked.

'It's just . . . you and Aastha are really close friends,' Rahul said.

Sameer frowned. 'Do you think that just because I'm friends with Aastha, I have to do everything she does?' he asked, a little insulted.

Rahul's eyes widened and he said hastily, 'No, that's not

what I meant at all! Look, I'm sorry. Can you just forget I said anything?'

'No, I can't,' said Sameer, leaning forward. 'Why would you think that?'

'It's just—she's kind of . . . a forceful personality, isn't she? I mean, not necessarily in a bad way; most of the time, it's great that she's so confident and strong. But she can be very set about some things and she doesn't hesitate to let people know what she thinks. And in this case, she's right, too—I have hurt Paddy. I just expected that you'd look at things the same way.'

'I guess I can see your point,' Sameer conceded. 'And you're right, she *is* a strong person. But she can also be very hard on people. The truth is, I've never been as principled as she is.'

Rahul frowned. 'Of course you are! You would *never* have done this to Karuna.'

'That's not what I meant,' he interrupted. 'It's just . . . Aastha's always had a lot of moral values which she would never compromise on. Which is fine, and I've always respected that, because there are some lines I would never cross, either. But the difference is that I don't expect the same of my friends and she does.'

Rahul made a face. 'Wow, now *that* makes me feel so great.'

'No, it's not like that,' Sameer clarified. 'I just meant that for me, friends come before my morals. So even though you really hurt Paddy, I won't just stop talking to you out of principle. I think it's more important to be a good friend.'

Rahul was moved by his words. 'I really thought I was going to lose all my friends over this,' he said. 'Thanks, Sam.'

There was a short silence and then Rahul remarked, 'I do

think that when it comes to Aastha, everything you just said would fly out of the window.'

'What do you mean?' he asked.

'If someone hurt her, you would definitely take sides.' He smiled a little. 'You've always been very protective of her.'

Rahul was right, that *was* the role he had played for Aastha, almost for the entire time he had known her. She had trusted him without reserve. How difficult must it have been for her that *he* had been the one to hurt her?

Rahul was frowning.

'What's wrong?'

'Nothing,' Sameer muttered, but it didn't sound convincing even to his own ears. 'You were saying?'

But Rahul didn't reply, he just studied him for a moment. 'I've been wondering,' he said, 'ever since Goa, you and Aastha have been acting strangely around each other. Did you guys have a fight or something?'

Sameer was caught off guard. He had thought he and Aastha had done a fairly good job of hiding things, but apparently Rahul was a lot more perceptive than he had given him credit for.

'I'm sorry,' Rahul said. 'I shouldn't have—'

'No, it's fine,' he interrupted. 'I just didn't think anyone had noticed.' He paused, wondering how much he should tell Rahul. 'It wasn't a fight. I, uh, did something, which hurt her. It was completely unintentional, of course, but it really shook her up. Since then, things have become really strained between us. We can't even talk to each other properly.'

'That really sucks,' Rahul said with feeling. 'The idea of you and Aastha at odds with each other is just *wrong*.'

'I know,' Sameer said morosely.

'Don't worry, you guys are too close not to fix it,' Rahul tried to reassure him. 'Just give it some time.'

Ironically, Sameer had told Rahul the exact same thing about Paddy, but he was just as unconvinced as his friend had been.

TWENTY

The past few weeks had been among the most trying Karuna had ever experienced. There were now only ten days left for Joseph's return to Bangalore and Sameer had still not told her what he had decided.

In the meantime, her parents were continually dropping hints and asking questions about Joseph. Her mother had even lingered near her bedroom door to eavesdrop on one of their phone calls one day, although Karuna had thrown such a fit when she saw her that she hadn't tried it again.

The worst part was that all the drama was affecting her concentration. Her exams were in three days, but she couldn't seem to focus. Her parents hadn't once asked her how her exam preparations were going. For years, they had pushed her to excel in her studies, but now it was as if the only thing that mattered to them was marrying her off.

It was a welcome relief when her phone rang and her heart lightened a little when she saw that Sameer was calling her. 'Hey, Sam.'

'Hey, what's up?'

'Oh, you know, trying and failing to study.'

'I have news,' he said. 'Paddy broke up with Rahul.'

'What?' Karuna exclaimed. 'When? Is she okay?'

'It happened this morning,' he said. 'Aastha's over at her house right now.'

'What happened, exactly?' Karuna asked.

'He got drunk and kissed Natasha at an office party.'

Karuna sat up, furious. 'That jerk!' she hissed.

Surprisingly, Sameer didn't immediately agree. 'He's feeling damn guilty about it,' he said. 'He told Paddy the truth the day after the party and he seems distraught over the whole thing. He's scared he's going to lose her for good.'

'He *should* be scared,' said Karuna. 'How do you know all this, anyway? Have you been hanging out with him?'

'He needs a friend right now,' Sameer said simply. 'And Paddy has you and Aastha. I'm not saying he did the right thing, but doesn't he need someone too?'

Karuna frowned. Her own loyalty was to Paddy first and her instinctive reaction was to yell at him. But she knew he had a point, so she forced herself to let it go. 'So how're things, otherwise?' she asked.

'Fine,' he said. 'You?'

Karuna breathed in deeply. 'My parents keep trying to find out how serious I am about Joseph. They want me to give them an answer.'

'Yeah,' said Sameer, a familiar wary note in his voice. She could sense he didn't want to talk about it. 'Listen, I have to run, I have work. I'll catch you later, okay?'

'You have work on a Saturday night!' she said flatly.

'Office has been pretty busy lately,' he said half-heartedly.

'And yet you have time to call me and tell me about Paddy's

break-up,' she snapped. *For how long was he going to keep avoiding this?*

'What, would you have preferred it if I didn't tell you?' he replied, irritated.

'I would prefer it if you actually talked to me about our relationship,' she said through gritted teeth. 'You can't keep running away from this!'

'I told you, I need more time to think!' said Sameer angrily. 'You can't just—'

'But I haven't *just* anything,' she interrupted. 'I've *given* you time. Joseph is getting here in ten days. I need to know your answer.'

'Why is it so important for you to know before he gets here?' asked Sameer. 'Would you really say yes to marrying him if I said no?'

'*Are* you saying no?' she countered.

'This is completely unfair,' said Sameer, frustrated. 'You're putting everything on me. You won't even consider refusing Joseph and dealing with the consequences.'

'I don't think you realize how difficult it is—'

'I don't fucking care,' he interrupted her. 'I'm tired of hearing that. It's not easy for me either. I'm supposed to give up all my career plans for you when you don't even have the guts to stand up to your parents?'

'I can't believe you just said that to me,' she said, her eyes filling. 'Again.'

'I don't like saying it,' he said with a little less heat. 'But it's the truth, isn't it?'

'I am willing to stand up to them,' she said. 'I'm willing to fight to marry you. It'll be hard enough trying to convince them to accept you as a son-in-law; I can't ask them to accept the idea of a boyfriend. It's too much.'

There was a long silence. 'I can't bear the thought of not being with you,' he said. 'But I can't be someone's husband yet.'

'Would it really be that different?' Karuna asked, not caring how desperate and pathetic she sounded. She could see where this conversation was headed and now she wished that she hadn't forced the issue.

'How could it not be?' he asked. 'It's not just a label, it's a huge responsibility. Everything I'd do, I'd have to keep you, your parents, your whole family, in mind. I can't handle it, Karuna.'

'But—' she began, but he wasn't finished.

'And that's not the only thing. I want to go abroad. Not just for an MBA, but a job too. It might be two or three years before I come back here, if I do at all. And you can't come with me when you're right in the middle of your actuaries.'

'I love you,' she said, her face wet with tears. 'Please don't do this.'

'Say no to your parents,' he countered shakily. 'Even if we break up, will you seriously be able to marry this guy? Will you really get over me that quickly, as if the last five years never happened, as if—'

'Shut up!' she interrupted, unable to bear thinking about it.

'Then just fucking stand up to them!' he said. 'How can you not have the guts to live your own life the way you want to?'

'I can't break their hearts like that!'

'But you're perfectly okay with breaking mine?' he asked bitterly.

'That's not fair,' she said heatedly. 'You aren't willing to give up your career for my sake, either. And if we're having this conversation, can we at least not end it shouting at each other?' Her voice broke.

'I'm sorry,' he said roughly.

They didn't say anything for some time, trying to postpone the moment when one of them would have to hang up. Then Sameer took a deep breath and said, 'I don't want to lose touch with you.'

'I don't either, but I need to get over you before I can talk to you again,' Karuna said. 'At least a year, I think.'

'A year?' Sameer said, hurt and shocked.

'It won't seem like a break-up if we keep talking all the time, Sameer,' she said.

'But . . .'

'It won't be forever,' she promised, swallowing hard. 'You've been a huge part of my life for a really long time and I don't want you out of it completely.'

'Even if you marry Jos—'

'I don't want to talk about that, Sameer,' she interrupted, her voice strained.

He was quiet for a long moment. 'I love you. I really do.'

Her eyes burned and she wished fiercely that she could see his face one last time. She was about to tell him that, but then her phone beeped in her ear, and she started to cry in earnest when she realized he had hung up on her.

———

She spent the next few days in a daze. By some miracle, she managed to get through her actuaries paper, but after that, she began to fall apart. Cooped up at home with not even the pressure of an upcoming exam to take her mind off things, she was plagued by the constant desire to call Sameer and beg him to reconsider.

Her parents made everything infinitely worse. Her father had no idea what had happened, while her mother's constant questioning broke her down. Together they made her feel more alone than she had ever felt before. And now she was supposed to meet Joseph. She had never dreaded anything so much, but was too tired to protest any further.

Her parents insisted that she wear her best clothes and she was driven in her father's Honda Accord to the restaurant, even though it was only a ten-minute walk from their house. As she rode the short distance, she kept thinking of Sameer and how he had asked her if she could bear to marry anyone else.

The car pulled up at the restaurant too soon, and she took a deep breath and got out. When she walked in, she had to scan the entire room twice before she spotted Joseph sitting at a tiny, easily overlooked table in the corner.

'Hey,' she said, making her way towards him.

'Karuna,' he said warmly, rising and shaking her hand. 'It's nice to finally meet you. You look just like your Facebook pictures.'

'Well, they *are* my pictures,' she pointed out, sitting down across from him.

'Yeah, but most girls Photoshop them to make themselves look much prettier than they really are,' he said and then backtracked. 'Um, I didn't mean—'

'It's fine, I'm not offended.'

'So how was your paper?'

'Decent,' she said. 'What about you, how has it been getting back here? Are you still jet-lagged?'

'Yeah, but it'll be okay in a few days,' he said dismissively. 'I'm going to miss New York; I had a great time there. Comic Con was awesome.'

'Yeah, you told me,' she said, feeling more at ease.

She didn't know why she had been so worried; this was no different from talking to him over the phone. When she left the restaurant, she realized that she had actually enjoyed herself. She was forced to admit to herself that she had begun to see him as a friend.

But she wasn't in the least attracted to him and the thought of marrying him, or anyone other than Sameer, was still unimaginable. She was also very aware of the fact that in all her conversations with Joseph, neither of them had mentioned the reason they were meeting in the first place. There was a chance that, like her, he was only doing this to humour his parents.

She sighed, feeling completely drained by so much thinking and worrying.

TWENTY-ONE

In the days that followed her break-up, Padmini found herself torn between fits of rage and crushing misery. She had always thought of herself as a reasonably strong person, but the past year had shattered her illusions. She had tolerated so much from Rahul and, even now, though she had sworn she wouldn't talk to him again, not a day went by that she didn't call him, either to scream at him or to cry.

Her appetite had diminished completely and she had to force herself to eat her meals. She was also nauseous all the time.

Rahul seemed deeply shaken by what he had done. He kept asking her to take him back and was obviously consumed by guilt. Even though she hated him for his betrayal, some part of her recognized that he could easily have kept it from her. She didn't know if she was grateful, or if she would rather not have known.

Aastha called and texted her regularly on weekdays and visited every weekend. Making so much time for her must have taken considerable effort and Padmini was grateful for it, but sometimes, Aastha's behaviour infuriated her.

She made no secret of her annoyance with Paddy for her constant need to talk to Rahul. She kept trying to take her phone away, making her feel like she was still in school. She knew Aastha was acting out of concern, but it began to grate on her nerves.

About two weeks after the break-up, Rahul called her and asked her to come and meet him for dinner. He said he missed her too much and wanted to at least stay friends with her. She reacted violently, told him he was completely over the line for even suggesting it, and hung up.

But after fifteen minutes, she began to reconsider and felt disgusted with herself for doing so. Was she really so dependent on Rahul? Upset, she called Karuna.

'Hey, Paddy,' said Karuna, rather dully. 'What's up?'

Padmini had called Karuna to vent about Rahul, but there was something very off about Karuna's tone. 'You sound really tired,' she said, concerned.

'Just going through a lot of shit,' she said.

'Sameer still hasn't given you an answer about the whole marriage thing?' asked Padmini.

'He did give me an answer, but it wasn't the one I wanted to hear,' said Karuna. 'We broke up.'

'Wait, what?' said Paddy, sitting up with a jerk. 'When did that happen?'

'The day after you broke up with Rahul, actually,' said Karuna. 'I'm surprised you didn't know that. I thought Sameer would definitely have told Aastha.'

'Are you okay?' Paddy asked. 'I mean, stupid question, obviously you're not, but how miserable are you?'

'I'm going crazy here,' she confessed. 'I met Joseph a couple of days ago and now my parents want me to meet him again. I don't know what to do; there's no way I'm ready to marry this guy. But I don't think my parents are going to give me an option here.'

'Wow,' said Paddy, stunned. 'And I thought *I* had problems. So you've really broken up with Sameer, then? I mean, you're not in touch at all?'

'No,' said Karuna. 'I do feel tempted to call him sometimes, but I don't want to put myself through that. I don't think there's anything more to say to him at this point. What about you, how are you doing? I know I should have called you, but I've had a lot on my mind.'

'I feel so betrayed,' said Padmini, a catch in her voice. 'Rahul and I have talked every single day since we broke up. I yell at him, he apologizes and begs me to take him back, and then I tell him never to call me again and hang up. But of course he does, or I call him, and then it's the same thing all over again. And I know it's ridiculous but I can't help it. I'm just so used to calling him and seeing him every day . . .'

'Are you thinking of taking him back?' Karuna asked.

'I'm damn confused,' Paddy admitted. 'I know I shouldn't be. He's treated me like shit; I shouldn't even be talking to him. Aastha keeps yelling at me for being so pathetic. But she doesn't get it, you know?'

'I know,' said Karuna. 'I was furious when I heard he cheated on you. But I can understand why you're so confused. It really is a lot to give up.' Her voice wavered and caught on the last sentence.

'Sorry,' said Padmini guiltily. 'I don't mean to make things worse for you.'

'Don't be silly,' said Karuna dismissively. 'You know you can always call me.'

'He wants to meet for dinner tomorrow,' Padmini said after a short pause. 'Do you think I should go?'

'I think you should do whatever you need to do to make yourself okay with this, one way or another,' said Karuna. 'If you think you can ever get over the whole cheating thing, then give him another shot. Otherwise let him go to hell and move on with your life, no matter how hard it is.'

'I don't know if I can ever get over his cheating on me,' said Padmini, feeling helpless. 'But I'm not ready for him to be out of my life completely, either.'

'Don't be like one of those couples who have broken up but not really broken up, you know? You'll just be in limbo if you do that.'

'Yeah, you're right,' said Padmini. 'Thanks.'

'Any time.'

Padmini wanted to ask about Joseph and if Karuna really was considering getting married to him, but she could sense, somehow, that Karuna didn't want to talk about it. So she let the conversation drift to other topics.

Finally, Karuna said, 'Hey, my mom's calling me for dinner. I have to go.'

'Oh, okay,' Padmini replied. 'I'll talk to you later, then.'

'Yeah, see you.'

She hung up. Padmini stared at her phone, now feeling even more confused about whether or not she should meet Rahul. Finally, she made up her mind and texted him.

Aastha was growing sick with worry. She had called Paddy three times, but her friend still hadn't responded. Paddy had been a complete mess since her break-up. Aastha was concerned that something was seriously wrong. She wanted to talk about it with Sameer, but she hadn't spoken to him at all since that awful awkward dinner. He had made no move to contact her, either.

She tried Paddy's number again and, this time, her friend picked up on the first ring. 'Hey, this isn't really a good time,' she said, obviously preoccupied. 'Is it important?'

'I was worried,' said Aastha. 'You weren't picking up.'

'Sorry, I'm out.'

'With whom?' Aastha asked. 'Don't tell me you're attending a book launch.'

Paddy hesitated. 'No, I'm actually on my way to meeting Rahul,' she said reluctantly. 'We're having dinner.'

'You're what?!' Aastha exploded. 'That is *not* a good idea!'

'I know he was a jerk with me, but we were together a long time,' said Paddy defensively. 'I wanted to meet him just this once. If nothing else, at least we should have a clean break after so many years, like Karuna and Sam.'

'Wait, what?' Aastha asked, unsure if she'd heard correctly. 'Karuna and Sam broke up? When?'

'Two weeks ago.'

'You never mentioned that!' Aastha exclaimed.

'I only found out a few days ago,' said Padmini. 'I thought you would know. Didn't Sameer tell you?'

'No, he didn't,' said Aastha, her eyes stinging. She had thought she would be relieved if Sameer decided not to marry

Karuna, but instead, all she could feel was hurt that he had kept this from her.

'Is everything okay between you guys?' Paddy asked. 'You haven't even mentioned him in the last couple of weeks.'

'We're fine,' said Aastha. 'Just . . . let me know what happens with your dinner.' She hung up before Paddy could ask any more questions.

She wanted to call Sameer and ask him how he was, ask him why he hadn't called her and told her about his break-up, but she didn't know if she should. He obviously hadn't wanted to speak to her. After thinking about it for a while, she realized that she was being ridiculous. They had been friends for too long for her to hesitate when he was probably going through one of the worst periods in his life. Taking a deep breath, she dialled his number.

———

Rahul watched Paddy pause outside the restaurant they had agreed to meet at. It was the first time he had seen her in two weeks and he couldn't take his eyes off her. He hadn't realized how fiercely he had missed her. She looked so tired and drained, and her frame was thinner than the last time he had seen her. It made him sick with guilt.

He rose to greet her when she entered. 'I'm really glad you came.'

'I'm still not sure I should have,' said Paddy, sitting down opposite him. 'I know Aastha's going to give me hell when I get home.' Her voice took on a self-deprecating tone. 'And I can see her point. Honestly, it *is* kind of pathetic that I would agree to meet you after what you did.'

He felt a familiar flicker of irritation—*what the hell did it matter what Aastha thought of the situation?* But he quashed the emotion. Now wasn't the time to get into that. 'I don't think you should think of it as pathetic,' he said carefully. 'If we were married, we would still have tried to make it work, wouldn't we? And no one would have called that pathetic.'

'We're not married, though!' she shot back. 'I'm twenty-four. Give me one good reason why I should put up with this shit.'

'Because you've been miserable without me,' said Rahul steadily. 'And because we're so used to each other, we can't even picture ourselves with anyone else.'

'I don't think being used to each other is a good enough reason,' she said. 'Aastha says you're like a bad habit I can't break.'

Rahul flinched, because that actually hurt. 'Aastha can go screw herself,' he said heatedly. 'Why do you always let her influence you?'

'Aastha's never let me down the way you have,' said Paddy angrily. 'Don't talk about her that way.'

'Paddy, you yourself get annoyed by the amount she interferes,' said Rahul, pleading. 'Can we not bring her into this? I want to talk to *you* right now, not her.'

Paddy sighed, making a visible effort to let go of her anger. 'Fine,' she said.

'I've really missed you,' said Rahul. 'I want you to give me a chance to make things right.'

'I really, really want to,' said Paddy. 'But I just don't know if I can ever trust you again after what you did.'

He swallowed hard. 'I know that. But we haven't really ended things, even now. Calling each other every day—we've not really broken up at all.'

Padmini shook her head. 'Karuna said the same thing. She told me I should meet you, if only to make a clean break.'

'Is that why you're here?'

'I don't know. I thought it was, but now—' She broke off, looking torn.

'I'm willing to do whatever it takes to make this up to you,' he said. 'I stopped talking to Natasha and I'm trying to find another job.'

'You are?' she said, her eyes widening in surprise.

'Yeah,' he said. 'I've been thinking about doing it for a while, anyway. It was a good place to start, but there are a lot of other places which would pay better. And I know you won't want me working in the same office with her. It might take time, but I really am trying.'

'That's . . . I don't know what I'm supposed to think about this,' she said. 'A few months ago, I would have welcomed it. But now, it's almost like you're doing it because you're scared of losing me and not because you're actually sorry.'

For a moment, he could only stare at her. 'You really think I'm not sorry?' he asked. 'You don't know how much I *hate* myself for what I did. I thought I had changed after college, I thought I knew better—' His voice broke.

'I didn't mean it like that,' she said. 'I know you're sorry—I knew it the day you told me. But it doesn't change how badly you hurt me. I haven't been sleeping, I barely have any appetite and, when I do eat, I throw up.'

He stared down at the table, blinking back tears. He

had already known all this, but hearing her say it aloud was heartbreaking. He was startled when she reached across the table and grabbed his hand.

'I'm not saying all this to hurt you,' she said softly. 'I just want you to understand where I'm coming from. I need to do what's good for me right now, and I'm not sure if you are any more.'

'I get that,' he said. 'And I can promise that I won't let you down again, but that's not going to make any difference to you. *You* have to make this decision. But I wish you'd stop listening to Aastha—I *don't* think it's a bad thing that we've become a habit. I think that would happen anyway, with anyone, whether you're twenty-three or forty. I want this to be your decision, not hers.'

'Fine,' she conceded, sighing heavily. 'But I need some time to think about it and I can't do that if we keep talking to each other. Can you hold off on calling me for a few weeks? And I will too.'

'If that's what you want,' he said sadly.

She nodded and they finished the rest of the meal in silence.

TWENTY-TWO

Sameer spent the days after his break-up oscillating between bouts of misery and the surreal feeling that nothing about his life had really changed. He and Karuna had been in a long-distance relationship for nearly a year, so he had gotten used to not meeting her. There were times when everything seemed fine; normal even. He would forget they had broken up and want to text or call her, and that was when it hit him.

He had looked up Joseph on Facebook the day after his break-up with Karuna. It had hurt to find his name on Karuna's friend list. He had gone through all of his profile pictures, his heart pounding in his chest, and tried to picture receiving a wedding invitation from them. But he couldn't—he honestly didn't think that she would be able to say yes to him. After all, he couldn't picture himself seriously dating anyone in the near future.

He often found himself wanting to call Aastha, but the memory of the awful dinner they had shared was enough to deter him. She hadn't tried to contact him since then, either, and that hurt him more than he cared to admit. Was one mistake enough to negate six years of friendship?

With Rahul and Paddy's break-up, their entire group seemed to have fractured. He barely saw any of his friends any more, except for Rahul. He wasn't much company though, since he was so miserable about Paddy. Sameer was hardly in a better frame of mind.

One night, when he was in a particularly black mood, Aastha called him unexpectedly.

'Sam?' she said, sounding very concerned. 'Are you okay? I just heard about your break-up. Why didn't you tell me?'

'You're kidding me, right?' he asked.

'What do you mean?' she asked, sounding hurt.

He knew deep down that he should stop himself, but he was feeling very bitter just then. 'I just think it's hilarious that you care so much about me all of a sudden.'

'Of course I care,' she said. 'Just because of . . . do you really think I would stop caring about you?'

'I don't know,' he said, frustrated. 'You refused to talk to me for weeks. I really needed advice and I thought I could count on you—'

'You know why I couldn't give you advice,' she said. 'Why are you being like this?'

Suddenly, he felt horribly guilty. 'I'm sorry,' he said. 'I didn't mean to lash out at you. I guess I've just been in an off mood.'

'It's fine,' she said, though she still sounded shaken. 'So, um, how are you?'

'I'm okay,' he said. 'I mean, obviously not completely . . . but I'm getting there, you know?'

'Yeah,' she said.

He could practically feel the tension crackling through the line and was suddenly furious with himself. She had reached out to him out of concern and he had ruined it by biting her head off. Desperate to recapture something of their old dynamic, he asked her, 'How are you these days? Have you been having nightmares?'

'What?' she asked, clearly caught off guard.

'You haven't called me in a while,' he said. 'I just wondered.'

'I'm fine,' she said stiffly, but it didn't sound very convincing.

His heart sank. His one constant fear since Goa had been the thought that he had set her back in her hard-won recovery.

'You'd tell me, right?' he asked, almost pleading. 'If you were having nightmares, I mean. I know things have been really weird between us lately and I know I didn't help matters by snapping at you just now. But you can still tell me anything— that hasn't changed.'

'Like you told me about your break-up?' she asked softly.

He flinched. 'Aastha, I—'

'It's fine, Sameer,' she interrupted hastily, obviously regretting her words. 'I know you had your reasons for not telling me.'

What reasons, he wondered, frustrated. She was the one who had been all strange and awkward whenever he mentioned Karuna.

'I'm going to hang up now, I have to eat dinner, but I'll see you later, okay?'

'Yeah, sure,' he said. 'See you.'

He hung up, feeling miserable. He knew he wouldn't be seeing her any time soon. He couldn't believe that in a few short months he had managed to lose not only Karuna, but Aastha, too. *How had his life gone to hell so quickly?*

Aastha stared at the computer screen, rereading the email she had just drafted. She couldn't concentrate.

Ever since her conversation with Sameer, she had tried to go on as if nothing had changed. And outwardly, nothing had—she still went to work every day, still worried about Padmini and checked on her regularly.

But even though she tried to pretend everything was fine, she was deeply shaken by the way Sameer had snapped at her when they had last spoken. He had never spoken to her like that in all the years she had known him and she couldn't forget about it.

Sometimes, she felt angry with herself for mooning over him like this. So many people crushed on their friends and carried on as if nothing had changed. Why couldn't she? Maybe if she'd had a more typical experience in college—had a boyfriend, hung out with friends, gone for an occasional drunken party, things would have been different. But the assault in F-Bar had changed her relationship with Sameer, turned it into something very intense. There was probably no one she trusted more unconditionally.

After that night in Goa, where she had experienced for the first time what it was like to be held by someone who loved her, whom she trusted completely. Every time she met him since then, or heard his voice on the phone, she could feel the warmth of his arms around her again. Was it any wonder that she couldn't pretend everything between them was unchanged?

She sighed and tried to refocus on her email. She was just finishing up when Nainika called her.

'Hey, what's up?'

'We're going out tonight. Route 69 again. Want to come?'

'Yes, please,' she said eagerly. Her social life had become almost negligible of late and the thought of spending time with someone other than Padmini was very appealing.

'Great,' said Nainika. 'Should I pick you up from work in an hour? Will you be done by then?'

'Yeah, sounds good,' she said.

The evening proved to be a welcome break—light, fun-filled conversation with friendly people who just wanted to have a good time after work. But the laughter and good-natured banter made her feel wistful, reminding her of the many Game Nights and dinners she had enjoyed with her own friends. Even though she was having fun, it still wasn't the same.

After her talk with Rahul, Padmini forced herself to stop calling him and began to think seriously about her future with him. Remembering her promise to him, she didn't tell Aastha anything about the decision weighing on her.

She realized that Rahul had been right—she *had* been allowing Aastha to influence her too much. Aastha had said so many times that Rahul was just a habit and had made her feel weak for needing to call him even after their break-up. It had never occurred to Padmini until Rahul had pointed it out that becoming that comfortable with someone might not be a bad thing.

When she thought about it, she realized that on some level, she already considered herself married to him. The thought should have scared her, but it didn't. Four years were four years, even if it wasn't formalized. Didn't she have an obligation to try and make things work, when they both had invested so much in this?

When she talked about it with Karuna, her friend understood her immediately. 'If that's how you feel, then you should try,' she said. 'What's making you hesitate?'

'I don't know if I'll ever be able to trust him again,' Paddy replied. 'I'm still so furious, you know. It makes me feel sick whenever I think about him cheating on me.'

'Well, I think you should give it a shot,' said Karuna. 'He seems like he's really sorry, from what you've told me. And if you find you just *can't* get over it, you can always break it off later. You still have that option.'

'Yeah, I know,' Padmini said. 'All this must sound completely trivial to you, right? I'm sorry I'm venting to you when you're going through so much yourself.'

'Don't keep apologizing for that,' said Karuna softly. 'You know you can always call me if you need me, no matter what.'

'So how *are* things with you?' Padmini asked. 'Have you met Joseph again?'

'A few times,' said Karuna. 'It's so strange. Every time we meet, we get along so well. I feel like if I hadn't met Sameer first, I would have happily said yes to him. But the truth is, I'm not attracted to him at all.'

'That sucks,' said Padmini.

'Tell me about it,' she said. 'My parents keep acting as if everything is a done deal already. I even caught my mom looking over her old wedding jewellery the other day! But Joseph hasn't yet mentioned marriage, even though we've met three times. We meet for coffee, and we talk about everything else but that, and then we both go home. I don't know what I'm supposed to think.'

'It sounds like he's not completely sure about you,' said Padmini. 'Do you think his parents are pressuring him, too?'

'I wouldn't be surprised,' said Karuna grimly. 'The whole thing is such a mess.'

'Shouldn't you try to discuss it with him properly?' Padmini asked. 'I mean, if he hasn't brought it up, why can't you?'

'I should, I know I should, but it just doesn't happen,' said Karuna. 'Every time I try, I get scared. It just seems . . . too real, you know?'

Padmini felt considerably alarmed by her friend's words. It sounded like Karuna was in denial about her situation and she was afraid that if her friend continued to avoid what was happening around her, she would find herself marrying Joseph without ever having had a meaningful conversation with him.

'I know it's difficult,' she said carefully. 'But it already *is* real. Avoiding it isn't going to help anyone.'

'I know,' said Karuna, sighing. 'I'll try to bring it up the next time we meet.' But her voice lacked conviction.

Padmini wondered, suddenly, what Karuna's life would be like a year from now. Would she be married to someone she didn't love because she hadn't had the guts to say something when she should have? The thought was terrifying.

In that moment, Padmini promised herself that no matter what happened, she would never end up like Karuna. If she did get back with Rahul, she would make sure it was actually a conscious choice and not something she just *fell* into. After so many years, she owed herself—and Rahul—at least that much.

TWENTY-THREE

It was as if all the fight had gone out of Karuna after her break-up with Sameer. Her parents would tell her when to meet Joseph and even though everything inside her screamed in protest, she would go. She felt like a spectator watching from the sidelines as she lived out her life, and she felt powerless to do anything about it.

One day, after her eighth or ninth meeting with Joseph, she entered her house, feeling bone-weary and utterly hopeless. Her mother was waiting for her and there was a look in her eyes that put Karuna instantly on edge.

'How was your date?' she asked casually.

She recoiled instinctively at the word. 'Don't call it that. It's not a date.'

Her mother looked surprised at her intensity, but let it pass. 'Whatever you want to call it. How was it?'

'It was fine,' she said vaguely, wanting nothing more than to escape the conversation. 'We get along well, whatever.'

She realized belatedly it had been the wrong thing to say. 'You get along well?' her mother repeated sharply, a gleam in her eye. 'That's wonderful, darling. We're thinking of calling his parents over for dinner this Friday.'

Karuna stared at her mother, horrified. 'You're what?' she exclaimed. 'You can't do that!'

'Of course we can,' said her mother. 'We probably should have, already. We agreed with his parents that we should give you both some time to get to know each other, but now it's been more than a month.'

Dread washed over Karuna. Meeting Joseph's parents was only one step away from deciding on an engagement date. 'Amma, please,' she pleaded. 'I don't want to get married. Please don't—'

'Oh Karuna, not again,' her mother interrupted. 'I've been so proud of you the last few weeks for finally being sensible. Please don't start creating trouble again, not now when things are falling into place.'

'I'm not creating trouble and nothing is falling into place!' Karuna retorted. 'Please, Amma, I'm not *ready* for this. I *don't* want to get married to him.'

Her mother pursed her lips. 'If this is about that boy again—' she began.

'Do you really think it's a good idea to get married to someone when I'm still in love with someone else?' she interrupted. 'That wouldn't be fair to anyone involved.'

Her mother shook her head. 'All these movies you watch have filled your head with nonsense,' she said impatiently. 'Stop being dramatic. You can take my word for it, when you get married, all of this will stop mattering. Joseph is a good boy. In a few months of being married to him, you will have forgotten all about your Sameer.'

Karuna stared at her mother and a wave of helplessness crashed over her. No matter what she said or did, her parents would never understand her. They were so sure that they knew what was best for her that they would always refuse to consider her feelings.

Even if she told Joseph the truth and broke things off, it still wouldn't solve her problem. She would eventually have to get married to the guy her parents chose. And Karuna knew that Joseph was probably the best she would get—someone like-minded and modern, with whom she could actually get along.

It was the first time she had acknowledged the possibility of marrying Joseph. Now, she pictured living with him every day, waking up beside him, kissing him—but that last thought brought vivid memories of Sameer. She had never been physically intimate with anyone else. What if she thought of him when she and Joseph had sex, or found herself comparing them? Or worse, what if she woke up one morning with Joseph's arms around her and said Sameer's name by mistake?

The thought made her feel sick and unhappy. She didn't know what to do. She turned and walked away from her mother, her mind whirling with confused thoughts.

As she wavered in limbo, her parents went ahead and made decisions for her. They carried out their plan of calling Joseph's parents over for dinner, and Karuna suffered through an evening of polite conversation and thinly veiled scrutiny. The only consolation was that Joseph seemed just as miserable as she was.

A week later, it was Joseph's parents who invited her family to their house for dinner. Joseph's mother asked her what she was planning to do in the future. She muttered something about working in an asset management firm. After that, she had asked about her actuary exams and how many papers she had cleared, with more interest than even her parents had shown.

Towards the end of the meal, Joseph's father asked her, very casually, 'Do you know how to cook?'

Karuna stared at him in shock, unable to believe he had actually asked her that. It was like something straight out of a Hindi movie. Out of the corner of her eye, she saw Joseph shrink visibly in his chair, a look of embarrassment on his face.

After a short pause, Karuna recovered herself and replied very pointedly, 'Not at all. I've even managed to ruin Maggi, on occasion.'

Joseph's father looked taken aback by the blunt reply and Karuna's parents shot her horrified looks. Joseph's mother quickly changed the subject and the dinner crawled on. By the time they left, Karuna was completely exhausted. She wanted nothing more than to sleep, but her parents followed her to her bedroom.

'You were very rude and barely answered any of the questions they asked,' her mother scolded. 'You have to be more careful about the impression you create. You're young, you don't realize, but these things matter so much after marriage.'

'I can't believe he asked me if I knew how to cook,' said Karuna, still seething. 'What does he think, that I'm going to cook and clean for Joseph? I'm just as educated as he is and I'm doing the actuarial exams.'

Her father scowled. 'When you get married, you will be expected to know these things by your in-laws.'

She lost her temper. 'First of all, Appa, I don't even *want* to get married to him. And even if I did, I'm *not* going to cook and clean for him. You can tell that to his parents or you can all go fuck yourselves for all I care.'

There was a ringing silence after the words. Her father, looking deeply hurt and offended, turned and walked out of the room without another word. Her mother's eyes were full of tears. 'I never thought I would see the day when my only child would speak to me that way,' she said. 'We are only telling you all this for your own good, why can't you understand that?'

'Why can't you understand this isn't what I want?' Karuna said desperately. 'Doesn't that matter to you?'

'Of course it matters,' said her mother. 'But we have to fulfil our duty as your parents.'

She turned and walked out of the room, leaving Karuna trembling with anger.

———

Two days later, she met Joseph for coffee again. This time, Karuna decided that enough was enough.

When there was a lull in the conversation, Karuna said abruptly, 'So, we need to talk about this.' She gestured between them. 'From what I can see, our parents are getting pretty serious and we haven't discussed it at all.'

Joseph looked for a moment like a deer caught in the headlights of a car and then he sighed, his shoulders slumping. 'I had a feeling this would come up,' he said. 'After that godawful dinner . . .'

'It seems like you're about as keen to get married as I am,' said Karuna.

'I don't want to give up my independence,' said Joseph. 'But, well, my parents have been on my case for two years now and, frankly, you're the only girl I've met who's even bearable.'

'Gee, thanks,' said Karuna dryly.

'I didn't mean—'

'I know what you meant,' she interrupted. 'I don't want to get married, either. I mean, I'm twenty-four, for God's sake.'

'So your parents are putting a lot of pressure on you?'

'Yeah.' She hesitated. 'I don't suppose you could tell them you don't like me so we can both get out of this?'

He snorted. 'I've been doing that from the beginning,' he said. 'It's not like they ever bloody listen.'

'I need to tell you something,' said Karuna. 'I have no idea how to cook and I have no intention of learning any time soon. I have to focus on studying. Also, if we do get married, I want to work. And I don't want to live in a joint family.'

'Dude, of course you can work,' said Joseph. 'My family isn't that orthodox. And I don't want to live with my parents either—they'd drive me crazy. As for the cooking thing, I don't care a damn about that. I'm earning well enough to afford a cook.'

Karuna let out a relieved breath. Perhaps this wouldn't be so bad after all, she thought. If she had to get married, this was probably the best she was going to get.

The only thing that kept nagging at her was the thought of Sameer. It was high time she told Joseph about that, but she'd have to choose her words carefully. 'You told me about Tanya in our very first conversation. I never told you that I had a boyfriend, too. We broke up less than a year ago.'

Something in his expression flickered, but it was gone

before she could decipher it. She waited for him to question her further, but he didn't. 'I think I should warn you,' he said after a pause. 'My parents are going to do an official proposal in a few days.'

'Really?' she asked, shocked. 'That's . . . really soon.'

'I know,' he said. 'But they think we've been seeing each other a lot and it won't be appropriate if we keep doing that without some formal agreement. They want to come to your house and exchange gifts and, then, you know, tell the extended family.'

She stared at him. After her relatives found out, there would be no going back. Could she really go through with this? She thought of telling her parents she wouldn't do it, of the tears and the recriminations that would be sure to follow. Then she thought of Sameer and how much she still loved him. She found herself blinking back tears.

'I know it's a lot,' Joseph said. 'Are you okay?'

She met his gaze, and saw her hesitation and fear reflected in his eyes.

She let out a shaky breath. 'I'm fine,' she said. 'Let's do this.'

TWENTY-FOUR

It was Friday night. Rahul sat alone in his apartment, staring
at the date on his phone. There were two days to his and
Padmini's five-year anniversary, and he still hadn't heard
from her.

When she had said she needed time, he had thought it
would only be a week or so before she called him. But it had
been a month already without even a text message from her.
If it weren't for Facebook, he would have had no idea what
was going on in her life.

He had kept his word not to call or text her, but it was so
hard. Not a day had gone by when he didn't miss her fiercely,
but Paddy seemed to be getting along fine without him.

He tried to focus his energies on finding a new job. So far
he had managed to get a few friends who were also working in
financial firms to recommend him to their HR teams. HSBC
had called him for an interview, but there were five more
rounds he would have to get through before he was selected.
Not that it mattered—he had stopped acknowledging Natasha
completely and would continue to avoid her whether or not
he got another job.

In the meantime, his weekends had become uneventful. Apart from spending time with Sameer, he had no one to hang out with. He missed the weekly Game Nights they all used to enjoy so much. Sighing, he got up and shuffled towards his bedroom.

He was about to call it a night when his phone rang. He froze when he saw Paddy's name flashing on the screen. *Was she finally breaking up with him?* He forced himself to pick up.

'Hey,' she said, more warmly than he had expected.

'It's really good to hear your voice,' he said. 'I've missed you.'

'I've missed you, too,' she said. 'We need to talk. Is it too late for you to come over?'

His heart began to pound wildly. 'Are you . . . are you breaking up with me?' he asked, fearfully.

'No,' said Paddy. 'I've been miserable over the last few weeks. I don't know if this is really stupid of me, but I want to give this another shot.'

He closed his eyes in relief. 'Thank you. You have no idea how . . .' He swallowed hard. 'I'll be right over.'

His heart singing, he drove the short distance to Padmini's apartment at breakneck speed. She flung her front door open seconds after he rang the doorbell and embraced him fiercely. He returned the hug with equal fervour, his eyes stinging.

'I love you,' he said roughly. 'I was so afraid I had fucked this up too badly to fix. I promise I won't mess up again.'

'You'd better not,' she said into his shoulder. 'Because I'm not giving you another chance.'

They broke apart after a few minutes and went into the house. Paddy sat down on the living room sofa and he sat beside her, clutching her hand tightly. 'What finally made you decide?' he asked after a pause.

'Our anniversary,' she said. 'Just the thought of five years . . . I couldn't bring myself to throw it away.'

'I was thinking about our anniversary, too,' he said.

She gave him a small smile and then said earnestly, 'Look, I know you're really relieved and so am I. But Rahul, this isn't going to be an easy fix. I'm still not sure I'll ever be able to trust you fully again, but I do want to try.'

'I can accept that, Paddy,' said Rahul steadily. He felt, in that moment, as if he could accept anything now that they were back together.

But Padmini wasn't convinced. 'You had said that after Purnima too,' she pointed out. 'But you lost patience pretty quickly when I started asking you too many questions about Natasha. What if that happens again?'

'I won't give you any reason to ask questions,' he said. 'I promise. I already know what it's like to lose you. I'm not going to mess this up again.'

They stared at each other for a long moment, until Padmini's gaze softened. 'Okay,' she said.

Elated, Rahul leaned in to kiss her. She responded eagerly and, for a few minutes, he focused on the familiar taste of her lips and tongue, until her hands snuck under his shirt and lightly caressed his back.

He moaned softly and broke away from the kiss, reaching for the hem of her shirt. She raised her hands above her head and allowed him to pull her shirt off, exposing her breasts. His mouth went dry.

Sliding his hands up her torso, he leaned forward to suck

on her neck. Her hands tightened against his skin when his hands cupped her breasts. When he ran his thumbs over her erect nipples, she gasped.

She began to stroke him through his jeans, sending sparks of pleasure jolting through his body. Taking his cue from her, his hand slid lower, and he was pleased to find that she was already wet.

'We should move—to the—bedroom.'

'Why?' he asked. 'I can think of plenty of things we can do right here on this sofa.'

Giving her a playful grin, he slid down the length of her body until he was kneeling before her. 'Are you . . . ?' she asked, surprised. It wasn't often that they did this for each other.

He gave her a slow warm smile. He wanted to make her feel as good as he possibly could, tonight. 'You bet I am,' he said.

———

Later, they lay together in bed, exhausted and happy. Padmini snuggled against his chest, her long hair tickling his face. 'I love you,' he whispered in her ear, his heart full.

'Love you too,' she mumbled.

He slept better than he had in months.

———

Padmini woke up feeling happier and more at peace than she had done in a long time. She opened her eyes and smiled as she felt Rahul's arms around her. For a while, she savoured the feeling of being so close to him, but she couldn't ignore nature's call for very long.

She tried to move from under his arms without waking him, but he was so tightly wrapped around her that it was a failed attempt. He blinked at her in confusion. 'What—where are you going?' he mumbled.

'Just the loo,' she whispered, pressing a kiss on his forehead reassuringly. 'Go back to sleep.'

When she emerged from the bathroom, she found him sitting up in bed, rubbing his eyes. 'Good morning,' she said. 'Sorry I woke you.'

'It's cool,' he said with a yawn. 'It's already eleven, anyway.'

'Seriously?' It had been a long time since she had slept so late.

'Yeah,' said Rahul. Stretching, he got out of bed and padded towards the bathroom. 'So what are we doing for breakfast?'

'Hungry?' she asked. 'I'll get started on French toast.'

She was quite hungry herself. She hummed under her breath as she pottered about in the kitchen for the eggs, milk and bread. It had been so long since she had cooked anything for anyone.

'Hey, need any help?' Rahul's voice made her jump.

She smiled and turned towards him. 'Nothing, I was just looking for the mixing bowl,' she said.

'It's right there,' he said, pointing to the washed dishes next to the sink.

'Oh, yeah,' she said, reaching for it, but he beat her to it.

'Here, I'll do it.' A pause. 'I mean, I'll mix the stuff after you, you know, put it in the bowl.'

She shook her head at him fondly—he really was hopeless in the kitchen. She broke the eggs into the bowl, added sugar and milk, and handed it to him with instructions to beat the eggs until she told him to stop. 'And do it gently, I don't need egg yolk spilling all over my counter.'

As she watched him, she remembered that she had forgotten to add salt, which was in an upper cupboard of the kitchen. She had to stand on tiptoe to reach for it, which caused her shirt to ride up, exposing her waist. She could feel Rahul's gaze on her and rolled her eyes. *Was he seriously this horny?*

She was about to tell him to focus on the eggs, when he said, in a slightly strangled voice, 'You've become so thin.'

'It's not that bad,' she said, shifting uncomfortably.

'How often have you been throwing up?' Rahul asked.

'Not that often,' she said honestly. 'I just didn't have much of an appetite. Chill, at the most I lost two or three kilos.'

This did nothing to diminish the guilt on his face. 'You should have told me you were throwing up,' he said. 'I would have stopped seeing her if I had known how bad it was.'

'No, you wouldn't have,' said Padmini, more bitterly than she had intended. 'You would have thought I was making it up or exaggerating. Or you would have resented me for making you stop talking to her.'

Immediately, she wished she could recall her words. She had promised to try and forgive him after all. 'Look, I'm sorry. Can we not ruin the mood by talking about all this? I honestly feel hungrier right now than I have in weeks and that's all that matters. Are you done with the eggs?'

He let the subject drop. 'I think so,' he said, showing her the mixture in the bowl.

She glanced at it and nodded. He placed the bowl on the counter and she began to dip slices of bread into it. The room filled with the aroma of eggs being fried.

They made small talk as they ate, discussing the things they had missed out on in the past few weeks of non-communication. As she described the high-profile book launch she had attended the previous week ('I swear, the food was *so good*, you would have loved it'), she pretended not to notice the way Rahul was watching her eat, with anxious eyes, only relaxing after she had eaten her fourth slice of bread.

After that, he told her about his job search. She was disappointed when she realized it would be weeks before he could switch to a new company. The idea that he was still working in the same office as Natasha made her skin crawl. Even though she had told herself she wouldn't mention it, she couldn't help but ask, 'How do you act around her in the office? Do you still have to talk to her sometimes?'

'No,' he said immediately. 'We're in different departments.'

'But—she never wanted to discuss what happened with you?' she pressed him.

'After that night, she sent a long email apologizing to me,' he said. 'She said she hoped we could stay friends. I responded and told her it was as much my fault as it was hers, but I thought it was best if I stayed away from her. She sent me another email, but I didn't bother to read it. Thankfully, she hasn't tried to talk to me since then. We basically just ignore each other.'

Padmini nodded. She was relieved, but there was still a niggling doubt in her mind that he wasn't telling her the truth. After all, she would have no way of knowing if they talked every day.

She changed the subject, asking him about HSBC and what his designation would be if he got in, but mentioning Natasha had cast a pall over the conversation. She was beginning to realize that getting back together with Rahul hadn't fixed anything between them. Couldn't they have managed one morning just feeling happy and grateful to be back together?

————

For what felt like the tenth time that day, Aastha dialled Padmini's number. Again, no one picked up.

She had been trying to get in touch with her since the previous night—they'd made plans to meet that afternoon for lunch—but her friend was refusing to pick up her phone. After hours of getting no response, she got worried. *What if something had happened to her?*

She felt the sudden urge to call Sameer, but immediately quashed it. She knew she couldn't keep depending on him for every little thing. If Padmini didn't pick up her phone in the next hour, she would go to her house herself to check on her.

Trying to distract herself from her thoughts, Aastha forced herself to open her laptop and watch an episode of *Friends*. Halfway through it, her phone rang, Paddy's name flashing on the screen. Relieved, she picked up the phone.

'Hey, I've been trying to call you since last night!'

'I'm really sorry, I left my phone in the hall last night,' Padmini said.

Aastha closed her eyes. 'I was worried sick,' she said. 'Please don't do that again.'

'Sorry,' her friend repeated contritely. 'How come you were calling?'

'We were supposed to meet today,' Aastha reminded her.

'Oh, yeah,' said Padmini. 'I don't think I'll be able to make it.'

Alarm bells went off in Aastha's head. She could sense that something was up. 'Why not?' she asked.

'Uh, Rahul's over here,' said Padmini reluctantly. 'We got back together.'

'You what?' Aastha exploded. 'He treated you like dirt; he fucking *cheated* on you—'

'I know all that, but we've been together five years,' Padmini interrupted. 'I decided to give him another chance. He's genuinely sorry for what he did.'

'Yeah, like he was *genuinely sorry* after Purnima?' Aastha spat out, furious. The next time she saw Rahul, she was going to strangle him for worming his way back into Paddy's life again.

'Why do you always bring that up?' Padmini asked, irritated. 'Don't you think I've already thought of all this? If I can move past it, then it shouldn't bother you.'

'You always forgive him for everything,' said Aastha through clenched teeth. 'And every time he hurts you, I'm the one who has to pick up the pieces.'

Padmini exhaled loudly. 'Look, I know you're concerned,' she said gently. 'And I guess you have a right to be, after how much I've cried to you over the past few months. But I feel so much better now that we're back together. Things are going to be different this time, you'll see.'

Aastha closed her eyes. She wanted to scream at her friend again for being so pathetically *dependent* on Rahul, but she restrained herself. Paddy had obviously made up her mind and there was nothing she could do to change it.

'Fine,' she said, shortly. 'I do want to meet you sometime soon, though. I want to hear how exactly this happened.'

'Maybe next Friday?' Paddy asked. 'We could do Game Night, just like old times. I haven't seen Sam in ages.'

Although she had missed hanging out with her friends, Aastha was less than enthused by the prospect now. She could just picture an evening of awkward conversation with Sameer, while Paddy and Rahul remained completely wrapped up in each other. Besides, she wouldn't even be able to probe Padmini for details with Rahul there.

'Sure, sounds good,' she said reluctantly. 'I'll see you then.'

TWENTY-FIVE

Sameer took a swig of his beer and, out of the corner of his eye, watched Rahul do the same. His friend looked happier and more relaxed than he had seen him in a long time, which was only to be expected now that he had patched things up with Paddy.

He had expected Rahul to be too wrapped up in Paddy for at least a month to bother meeting him, but here he was. He eyed his friend speculatively, wondering what to make of it.

'What?' Rahul asked, frowning when he caught his gaze.

'Nothing, just kind of surprised you came over here today,' said Sameer.

'Why? I come over here all the time.'

'I know, I just thought you would want to spend all your spare time with Paddy,' said Sameer.

'I don't know,' said Rahul. 'I thought that, too, and I am ecstatic that we're back together. But it feels more as if everything's gone back to normal, rather than as if something amazing has happened. It's not *better*, you know? Just the same.'

'I hope you aren't fighting, at least,' Sameer said.

'No, not fighting exactly,' said Rahul. 'But she still gets really insecure about the fact that I'm working in the same office as Natasha.'

'Just give it time,' said Sameer. 'After all, it's only been a few months since—'

He was interrupted by the loud insistent vibration of his cell phone on the coffee table. He reached for it and froze in shock when he saw Karuna's name flashing on the screen. He'd had no communication with her since they'd broken up. Why was she calling him now? A wild fierce hope beat in his chest as he wondered if she wanted to get back together with him.

'Pick it up, idiot,' said Rahul as he continued to stare at his phone. 'I'm going inside.'

He sprang up from the beanbag he'd been sitting on, hurrying into Sameer's bedroom and shutting the door behind him. Swallowing hard, Sameer pressed the phone to his ear. 'Hello?'

'Hey, Sam,' she said. 'How . . . how are you?'

'I've been better,' he said honestly. 'It's really good to hear your voice.'

'You too,' she said.

He waited for her to say something, but she was silent. 'So, what's up?' he asked finally.

'I, uh, have some news,' she said reluctantly.

'What news?' he asked.

'I wanted you to hear it from me first,' she said in a small voice. 'Joseph and I . . . we're getting engaged next month.'

For a second, his mind went blank and he couldn't find the words to respond. Then, rage washed over him and he shot to his feet, shaking. 'You're *what*?' he shouted.

'Sameer, please,' she said. 'You knew this was coming.'

'Are you fucking serious?' he snapped, unable to believe her words. 'We barely broke up a month ago! And just like that, you're over it? You're ready to move on, marry someone else?' His voice cracked. 'Yeah, we were together only for five years, of course I should have seen this coming.'

'Of course I'm not over it!' she exclaimed. 'I don't *want* to do this, but I don't have a choice!'

The familiar words filled him with disgust. 'Yeah, you keep telling yourself that,' he said harshly. 'Maybe some day you'll actually fool yourself into believing it, but you don't fool me for a second. You've always had a choice. I hope you rot in hell now that you've made it.'

He hung up and slammed the phone down on the coffee table. His heart was pounding.

His bedroom door opened and Rahul stepped out cautiously. 'What happened?' he asked.

'She's getting engaged,' he said.

'Fuck!' said Rahul. 'I'm sorry, man.'

'Just the *thought* of going on a date would be unthinkable for me right now,' he said, his voice shaking. 'How can she do this? I never thought—I mean, I knew she was meeting Joseph, but I thought she'd find a way to get out of it, I thought she'd need *time* to get over me. But this—' He broke off, unable to find words to express what he was feeling.

Rahul squeezed his shoulder. 'I don't think she *is* over you,' he said.

'Yeah, well, that really doesn't make me feel better,' said Sameer.

In fact, that was even worse. How could she consider getting married to Joseph if she wasn't over him? He knew that with time *he* would eventually move on, date someone else, get married on his own terms. But Karuna wouldn't have that. He pictured her years from now, looking back on their relationship and blaming Sameer for not marrying her. He wanted to hop on a plane right then and fly to Bangalore so he could drill some sense into her.

To his intense shame, he found himself blinking away tears. He turned his face away, but not before Rahul had noticed. His friend looked at him in alarm. It was very rare for Sameer to get this upset.

'Are you—' he began.

'Fine, just give me a sec,' Sameer muttered, his face burning with embarrassment.

'Do you want me to call Aastha?' Rahul asked him quietly.

'God, no,' Sameer said, a little too quickly. The memory of their last painful conversation was still too fresh in his mind.

Rahul frowned. 'Come on, Sameer,' he chided him.

'I don't even know if we're that close any more,' said Sameer, though it hurt him to admit it. 'Things have been so fucked up since Goa.'

'You need to try and patch things up with her,' said Rahul. 'Maybe you could talk when we meet for Game Night tomorrow.'

The prospect of Game Night when he was already so miserable was suddenly very unappealing. 'Yeah, I don't know if I'm going to be able to make it,' he lied. 'I have some reports to submit which I haven't even started working on.'

'But you can't ditch Game Night!' Rahul protested. 'We won't be able to play anything good with only three people.'

'I'll try, but it doesn't look likely,' Sameer said. The conversation with Karuna had left him feeling completely hollow, so he added, 'I'm sorry, but I'm exhausted. I think I'm going to crash now, if that's okay.'

Rahul eyed him, concerned and sympathetic. 'Sure,' he said.

Sameer headed for his bedroom. He didn't even bother to change, just switched off the lights and sprawled on the bed. He wanted nothing more than to sleep, but it was a very long time before he managed to calm his whirling thoughts sufficiently.

———

Aastha rang Padmini's doorbell and tried not to scowl when Rahul opened the door.

'Hey,' she said coolly. 'Where's Paddy?'

'In the loo,' he replied with a guarded air. 'She'll be out in a sec. What do you want to play?'

'Anything, I don't care,' she said.

They stood in the living room awkwardly. 'I can't believe how long it's been since we had Game Night,' Rahul said after a few moments.

'Yeah, well, whose fault was that?' she muttered before she could stop herself.

His smile faltered and then he looked irritated. 'Aastha, I know you don't—' he began.

'Hey, Aastha!' Padmini emerged from her bedroom, towelling her hair dry. She was smiling a little too brightly. 'What do you think we should do tonight? I wanted to play Risk—it's been ages, but we need four people, and with Sameer not coming—'

'Wait, what?' Aastha interrupted. 'Why isn't he coming?'

'He said he had some report due which he hadn't even started working on,' said Rahul.

'That doesn't sound like him at all,' said Aastha, frowning. Sameer had always made an effort to come for Game Night, no matter how busy he was.

'Frankly, I don't think he's up for it, what with Karuna getting engaged.'

Aastha started. 'She's getting engaged?' she repeated, shocked. 'When?'

'Next month, apparently,' Rahul replied.

God, this would kill Sameer, she thought. A small shameful part of her was glad that Karuna was out of his reach for good, but she refused to acknowledge it. She thought of Sameer sitting alone in his flat, reeling from this latest heartbreak, and she ached to go over there and offer him words of comfort.

'I don't know what the hell Karuna's thinking,' Padmini was saying. 'She is so obviously not ready for this . . . it's insane.'

'Maybe you should call Sameer and talk to him about it,' Rahul suggested to Aastha. 'He seemed pretty upset yesterday.'

Aastha stared at him. 'You met Sameer yesterday?' she asked.

'Uh, yeah,' said Rahul cautiously, exchanging a look with Paddy. 'We've been hanging out a lot over the last two months.'

Aastha couldn't believe that it had come to this; even *Rahul* seemed more clued in to Sameer's life than she was. Padmini, sensing her darkening mood, changed the subject quickly. 'Maybe we could play a round of Taboo?' she asked.

'I'm starving, though, let's order first,' said Rahul. 'Pizza sound okay?'

'Sure,' said Aastha dully.

They ordered the pizza and then played a few rounds of Taboo. It was a rather dismal affair. With only the three of them, they couldn't even play in teams, so half the fun was lost. Aastha had too much on her mind to focus properly and kept making silly mistakes. She was relieved when the pizza arrived.

As they ate, she watched Rahul and Padmini quietly. They were acting as if they had never broken up in the first place. Padmini ate four slices, when, not even a week ago, she wouldn't even have been able to manage one. It was a relief to see her eating again, but Aastha couldn't help hating this fresh evidence of her dependence on Rahul.

TWENTY-SIX

Later that night, when Aastha disappeared into the bedroom, Padmini and Rahul exchanged dismayed looks.

'That could have gone better,' said Paddy, making a face.

'She didn't even make an effort!' Rahul exclaimed. 'And the way she kept glaring at me . . .'

'Yeah, well, it's obvious she hasn't forgiven you yet,' said Padmini, frustrated. 'I don't know why she always does this. If *I* could let it go, why the hell can't she?'

'She's just being overprotective, I guess,' said Rahul.

But Padmini shook her head in frustration. 'She doesn't have the right to comment,' she said. 'I feel like she's judging me all the time. Like I'm this pathetic doormat who lets my boyfriend walk all over me. But that's not true. I made a conscious choice to take you back and she has no right to judge me.'

'I know, Paddy,' said Rahul. 'Just let it go, she'll get over it.'

'What do you want to do now?' she asked. 'Should we watch a movie?'

'D'you have anything new?' Rahul asked.

'Not really,' said Paddy, racking her brains. 'Uh, I do have

199

the first couple of episodes of *The Newsroom*, though. I know you've been wanting to watch that for a while.'

They watched the first episode of the show and then took a break. Rahul opened his laptop and began to check his email, while Padmini went into her bedroom to retrieve a set of proofs. Catching sight of Aastha sleeping on the floor, she couldn't help but experience a fresh upsurge of exasperation. She had really been looking forward to the evening, hoping it would be a reunion of sorts for the four of them, but Aastha had completely ruined the mood.

Sighing, she tiptoed past her friend and made her way back to the couch. The next hour was spent in a companionable silence, interrupted only by Rahul's fingers tapping occasionally on the keyboard as he browsed the internet.

'I'm hungry,' said Rahul after a while. 'Do you have anything lying around in the kitchen?'

'Sure,' said Paddy. 'There's a packet of popcorn in the cupboard, could you make some? I want to finish editing this chapter.'

'Sure,' said Rahul, placing his laptop on the coffee table and rising.

'You do know how to make popcorn, don't you?' she called after him.

'It's ready-made, I'm not that hopeless.' A pause, then he called, 'I can't find it.'

'It's in one of the cupboards, just look for it,' she replied, rolling her eyes.

'Paddy, I still can't find it,' he said after a couple of minutes.

With a long-suffering expression, she rose from the couch and went to help him. She opened a few cupboards and rummaged till she found the packet. 'It's right here! You never look for things properly,' she chided him.

'Sorry,' he said sheepishly.

She handed him the packet and made her way back to the couch. Just as she was about to sit down, her eyes landed on Rahul's laptop screen. His inbox was open and she saw the name Natasha Khanna right on top. She froze for a moment and then moved closer to the laptop. Her blood boiled when she saw that there were eight or ten emails from her, right at the top of his mailbox. Acting on autopilot, she clicked on the email at the top of the list.

Abhi is giving me a really hard time. i thought i could count on ur support at a time like this.

She clicked on the mail below.

The next one read, *am getting sloshed almost every night, scared im drinking too much, i really need ur support right now.*

Hands shaking, she clicked on Rahul's 'sent messages' folder, and was relieved to find that he hadn't responded to any of the emails. But then some instinct made her check his drafts, too, and she was filled with anger when she saw that there was a half-composed mail in reply to the one Natasha had written.

Natasha, I'm really sorry to hear that you're having such a difficult time. I hope you—

'What the fuck are you doing?' Rahul's voice made her jump. She turned to see him glaring at her, the bowl of popcorn clutched in his hands. 'How could you read my emails?'

'You're a lying asshole,' she said, furious. 'You said you'd stopped talking to her and she's writing you emails now? I can't believe you—'

'I *have* stopped talking to her!' he interrupted angrily. 'Why do you think she sent me so many mails? She keeps begging me to respond—'

'If she's so desperate, I'm sure she's also tried to talk to you in office, which you must have *lied* about—'

'I didn't lie to you!' he shouted, setting down the popcorn and striding up to her. 'Have you forgotten I work in an open cubicle? If I ignore her in front of everyone else, or create a scene, it'd be too embarrassing for her, so she never tries to talk to me—'

'And I'm supposed to believe that, when you didn't even tell me about the emails!' Padmini retorted.

'I got them today! And I swear I didn't respond—'

'You were going to!' she shouted, jerking her hands towards the draft she'd been reading. 'You were sitting right next to me and you were writing an email to her. Do you know how *sick* that makes me feel?'

'She said she'd been drinking too much,' he pleaded. 'I couldn't just ignore that! I was just writing to tell her that—'

Padmini's temper snapped completely. She had never been so angry in her life. 'I don't fucking care,' she roared. 'I can't *believe* you could even try to justify this, I should have known better than to trust you, all it took was for her to play damsel in distress again and you went running back to her.'

'I didn't go running back to her,' Rahul said angrily, seizing her shoulders. 'Would you just listen for a second?'

'I don't want to hear anything you have to say!' she yelled, shoving at his chest in a blind fury.

'Paddy, stop, what the fuck are you *doing*—'

He grabbed her hands to try and restrain her. She tried to

wrench them away from him, but he was holding her so tightly that his hands followed the motion and the next thing he knew, one of his knuckles collided hard with her eye. She cried out in pain and he let her go as if he'd been burned.

For a moment, they both stood there, frozen. Then Rahul surged forward, a look of guilty horror descending on his face. 'Oh shit!' he said in a strangled voice. 'Are you okay?'

Before Padmini could reply, Aastha's voice rang out from across the room. 'What the hell is going on?'

Padmini stilled. She had only one moment to process what was happening before Aastha caught sight of her. She turned on Rahul furiously. 'You bastard, how could you hit her!'

'It was an accident,' said Rahul, shaken.

'I knew it; I knew it was only a matter of time before you hurt her again. You've always treated her like shit, but this is the limit!'

'Hey, it really was an accident,' Padmini said.

'Are you seriously defending him?' Aastha asked in disbelief.

Years of irritation at Aastha's constant interference suddenly coalesced and Padmini was furious again. 'Of course I am!' she exclaimed. 'You don't get to just come and scream at him without even knowing what happened. It was an accident, we were fighting and—'

'I don't need to hear it,' said Aastha, turning angry disappointed eyes on Padmini. 'I've seen enough of you two to know how this goes. He always treats you like shit and you always forgive him.'

'Well, I'm glad you're making your feelings about the subject so clear,' Padmini said with biting sarcasm. 'I mean, it's not like I asked you what you thought, but *of course* you have a God-given right to interfere in my relationship.'

Aastha looked hurt at the comment. 'I'm the one who was here every time he let you down,' she said. 'How many times have you cried on my shoulder, how many times have you whined about how he hurt you?'

'That doesn't give you the right to dictate my decisions,' said Padmini stonily.

'Every time he hurts you, you take him back,' Aastha continued as if she hadn't heard her. 'He cheated on you twice and you still took him back. Now he's hit you and you're trying to defend him. How much more abuse are you going to take before you decide it's enough?'

Paddy stared at Aastha in shock.

'You seriously think I'm capable of that?' said Rahul, shaken. 'You've known me for years. You seriously think I'm *abusive*?'

There was an ugly look on Aastha's face. 'No one has *ever* hurt her worse than you,' she said fiercely.

'You need to back off,' Padmini said. 'You don't get to say things like that to him. It's not your place and he doesn't deserve it.'

'Oh, of course you'd say that,' said Aastha, scoffing. 'Why am I even surprised? You know, now that I think about it, this is *definitely* an abusive relationship. This is exactly what abused wives do—*"Oh, it only happened once, it was just an accident"*—I don't know who the fuck you're even trying to convince.'

'I had no idea you thought so little of me,' said Paddy, shaking with anger. 'But I refuse to hear another word. You need to get the fuck out of here, or I'm going to lose it completely. No,' she said when Aastha tried to say something. 'I've had enough! Get the hell out of my house!'

Aastha turned and marched out of the door.

Aastha trembled and shook as she climbed down the stairs. Her movements felt heavy and uncoordinated, and her heart was pounding as if she had just run a marathon. Padmini's face swam before her, and it was all she could do not to turn and march back up the stairs, take her friend by the shoulders and shake her for being so *weak*.

She couldn't understand how Paddy could even consider staying with Rahul after everything he had done to hurt her. She hadn't meant to call him abusive, but when the words had left her mouth, she had felt chilled to the bone by the ring of truth they contained. She could easily envision that future for her friend and she shuddered at the thought.

She crossed the courtyard and reached the front gate. The street was completely deserted and silent. It was only then that she realized it was the middle of the night and she had no way of getting home. She had been so overwrought that she hadn't even thought of it and what hurt even worse was that Paddy hadn't thought of it either.

She stared at the empty street and then back towards Paddy's flat. She couldn't bring herself to go back up the stairs; her pride wouldn't allow it. A car drove past and she tensed, suddenly remembering all the rape cases that had been in the papers recently, how so many girls were pulled into cars by strangers.

She shuddered as that familiar never-forgotten sense of fear and vulnerability washed over her. Somewhere in the distance, she could hear the sounds of loud drunken laughter, followed by the strains of a popular Bollywood dance number played at high volume on a car's stereo system.

Her heart flip-flopped. She needed to get out of there. With shaking hands, she dialled for a Meru cab, waited agonizingly while they kept her on hold, only to be told that there were no cars available till the following morning. She stood there, wondering what to do. The only person she could think of calling was Sameer, but it would take him some time to get there. Besides, she didn't want to have to be 'rescued' by him, when everything between them was already so messed up.

For a few minutes, she stood there trembling, until another car passed, and her fear got the better of her. She dialled Sameer's number. She wondered if he was too deeply asleep to hear the call, although that had never happened before. Then just as she was about to disconnect, he picked up.

'Aastha?' he asked, sounding surprisingly alert.

'Hey,' she said shakily.

'Is something wrong?' he asked, concerned.

'I, uh, need you to come and pick me up from Paddy's,' she said, her voice cracking. 'I'm really sorry. I didn't know who else to call.'

'What the hell happened?' he asked.

'Can you just get here?' she pleaded.

'I'm on my way,' he said.

She stood there clutching her phone, trying not to listen to the sounds of cars passing as the minutes crawled by. She glanced back at Padmini's building, hurt that her friend hadn't called her back inside. She couldn't believe that she had been chucked out of the house in the middle of the night.

She heard the sound of a car's engine and tensed at its approach. It slowed down when it neared Paddy's gate and her heart leapt into her throat. She began to scramble backwards, shaking with fear.

'Aastha?' Sameer's familiar voice stopped her in her tracks and she nearly stumbled from the force of her relief. *How on earth had he gotten here so fast?*

She turned as he jumped out of the car, his expression drawn with worry. 'What's going on?' he demanded. 'Why are you out on the street? You should have waited inside.'

In that moment, she was so relieved to see him that she forgot all about the awkwardness of the last few months. She crashed into his arms, sobbing. He froze in surprise, but then he hugged her back, murmuring soothingly.

'Hey, hey, you're okay. Come on. Everything's fine.'

She hadn't realized till now how much she had missed him. She experienced again that sensation of feeling completely safe and loved, and she tightened her grasp on his shoulders. After a few minutes, he pulled away from her. 'Come on,' he said. 'Let's get you home.'

Soon they were speeding away from Paddy's house. Now that she was no longer so afraid, her tears stopped flowing incessantly. When Sameer saw she had calmed down, he asked her again, 'What the fuck happened, Aastha? Did you have a fight with Paddy or something?'

'Yeah, I guess you could call it that,' she said hoarsely. He waited for her to elaborate and she drew in a deep breath. 'Rahul hit her.'

Sameer was so shocked that he nearly swerved into the pavement. 'He couldn't have,' he stammered. 'He wouldn't do something like that.'

'He did,' she said. 'They were arguing and he lost control.'

He stared at her with wide disbelieving eyes. 'Tell me the whole story.'

———

When Aastha slammed the door shut, she left behind a ringing silence. For a while, Padmini just stood there, shell-shocked. Rahul was frozen too, struck dumb by the events of the evening.

After a couple of minutes, she could no longer ignore the throbbing in her left eye. She turned and made her way to the kitchen. She was grateful when Rahul made no move to follow—she needed the time to gather her thoughts.

She opened the fridge and fished a packet of peas out of the freezer, pressing it to her eye. Leaning against the kitchen counter, she drew in a shuddering breath. Never before had she had such an awful argument, either with Rahul or with Aastha. With Aastha, she didn't regret her anger. By calling Rahul abusive, she had completely crossed the line.

She was, however, horrified by how spectacularly her argument with Rahul had spiralled out of control. Thinking about it now in the quiet of the kitchen, she was forced to acknowledge that her lingering insecurities had probably made her jump to conclusions. She felt disturbed and ashamed of how violently she had reacted. They had gotten back together with such wonderful intentions of forgiveness and reconciliation, and within the very first week, they'd had such an explosive fight.

She stood there for some time, trying to gather her thoughts. Then, bracing herself, she walked out of the kitchen and back into the living room. Rahul was standing with his back to her, gazing out of the window at the street below.

She cleared her throat and he turned, his face stricken with guilt when he saw the packet of peas she still had pressed to her eye. 'I am *so* sorry,' he said earnestly, crossing the room and standing before her.

'Not your fault,' she said, feeling completely drained. 'I was trying to hit you.'

'Does it hurt?' he asked.

'Not that badly,' she said to spare his feelings.

'I wasn't lying to you,' he said. 'She sent me all those emails today. When I saw the one about the drinking, yeah, I was tempted to go and meet her, but it was only for a few minutes, and then I realized what a horrible mistake it would be. I was writing to tell her I was sorry she'd been drinking, but I couldn't get involved, and to please stop writing to me in the future. That was it, you have to believe me.'

Padmini did. 'I guess I feel really insecure that you're still working in the same office as her,' she admitted reluctantly. 'I shouldn't have checked your laptop like that.'

'The way you reacted, it was almost like you'd been *expecting* me to cheat again,' Rahul said, obviously troubled. 'Like it was only a matter of time. That's exactly what Aastha said, too. Do you really feel that way about me?'

'I . . . don't know,' said Padmini, faltering. When his face fell, she hastened to add, 'When I really think about it, I obviously know you aren't cheating on me. But I'd be lying if said I don't worry about it.'

'I have to wonder if Aastha had a point,' said Rahul. 'I can't believe I'm even saying this after I fought so hard to get you back, but is all of this even worth it? Our issues obviously aren't going to get resolved any time soon and I've already hurt you a lot. I don't want to hurt you any more.'

'Are you reconsidering us getting back together?' she asked in shock.

'I don't want to reconsider it,' he said unhappily. 'But if it's hurting you worse, maybe it's time I bow out.'

She forced herself to think about it honestly. 'Maybe I am a little insecure . . . and a little jealous,' she said slowly. 'Maybe we'll fight like this again, I don't know. I mean, obviously neither of us should ever get physically hurt again, but I can picture myself screaming at you and getting angry and possessive. But as long as we're always able to work through it like we're doing now, to discuss it and try to do better, I think I could accept a few fights.'

Rahul still looked unconvinced. 'What if you're never completely able to get past this?' he asked, his eyes boring into hers. 'What if five years from now you still get jealous when I'm out with a female colleague?'

'I hope that won't happen,' she said. 'But if it does, I'll scream at you and cry over it for a while,' she said. 'And you'll yell at me. And then I'll see I'm being stupid, and we'll work it out and move on, like we always do.'

As she spoke, she felt a sense of calm and certainty settling over her. In that moment, she could envision their future very clearly. They would argue, make up, move on, love each other, laugh, argue again, make up again—but always, always, they would try to move forward. It would never be perfect, but she would never be happy with anyone else.

For a long moment, he stared at her, searching her face intently until he found what he was looking for. And then he pulled her to him and kissed her. That was all the answer she needed.

TWENTY-SEVEN

The next morning Rahul was woken by the sound of his phone ringing. He reached for his phone, still half asleep. 'Hello?'

Sameer's voice sounded in his ear, angry and demanding. 'You want to tell me what the fuck happened last night? Please tell me you didn't actually *hit* Paddy.'

'Of course not!' Rahul exclaimed, suddenly wide awake, 'You really think I would do that?'

'Aastha said she *saw* you hit her,' said Sameer.

Paddy stirred beside him, mumbling in her sleep.

Not wanting to wake her, he left the room. 'Aastha didn't understand what she saw. It was an accident. We were arguing and Paddy pushed me. I tried to grab her hands to stop her and my hand got knocked into her eye. I feel guilty as hell about it, but it wasn't something I did on *purpose*. We tried to explain that to Aastha, but she wouldn't listen.'

'Oh,' Sameer said, relieved. 'That . . . makes more sense.'

'I can't believe you thought I could ever hit Paddy.'

'I didn't, that's why I'm calling in the first place,' said

Sameer. 'But I am really angry with you and Paddy for throwing her out in the middle of the night.'

'I had my eye on her the whole time!' Rahul protested. 'After I called you, I watched her from the window. She sort of stood there for a while and then she took out her phone and called someone—you, I'm guessing—and then you got there and she hugged you . . .'

'But it still wasn't safe to let her stand there on the street,' Sameer insisted. 'What would you have done if something had actually happened to her, even if you *were* watching?'

Rahul had to concede the point. But when he tried to picture calling Aastha back after she had stormed out, he couldn't see how that would have ended well, either. 'She and Paddy were so furious with each other, she wouldn't have agreed to come upstairs anyway.'

'Yes, she would have,' said Sameer. 'She was so terrified, she was shaking by the time I got there.'

Rahul felt a pang of guilt. 'Is she okay now?' he asked.

'She's sleeping now, but she was really upset,' said Sameer. 'From what I understood, she and Paddy had a really nasty argument, but she wouldn't give me the details.'

'She said some really awful things,' said Rahul. 'Obviously, Paddy was furious and told her she had no right to interfere, but she wouldn't back down. She called me abusive and she compared Paddy to an abused wife because she keeps taking shit from me.'

'She said what?' Sameer asked in shock. 'Fuck!'

'It was way over the line,' said Rahul. 'You need to talk some sense into her. She can't keep doing this.'

'I don't know,' said Sameer doubtfully. 'I'm not sure how much of an impact I'd even have. Like I said, we're not as close as we used to be.'

'Oh, don't give me that crap,' said Rahul, exasperated. 'She called you last night, didn't she? She might not listen to anyone else, but she *will* listen to you. She always does.'

'Well, I'll try, and see how it goes,' said Sameer. 'I'll catch you later, then.'

'Yeah, okay.' Rahul disconnected the call and stared down at his phone morosely. He was still very disturbed that Aastha had thought he was abusive. Even though he knew she had never thought him good enough for Paddy, he hadn't thought her distrust ran so deep. They had spent so much time together over the years, so many Game Nights, dinners, sleepovers. How could she have thought him capable of that?

'Hey,' Paddy's voice, still thick with sleep, interrupted his thoughts. 'Is everything okay?'

He turned and inhaled sharply when he caught sight of her eye. 'Fuck, it *actually* looks like I punched you.'

'It's nothing a little foundation won't take care of,' she said dismissively. 'Who were you talking to?'

'Sameer,' he said. 'He wanted to know what happened last night. Apparently, Aastha told him I hit you. He understood when I explained the whole thing, and I think he's going to try and talk to her.'

Paddy's expression had grown stony with anger again. 'I can't believe she told him that,' she muttered.

'He was also really angry with us for chucking Aastha out in the middle of the night,' Rahul continued. 'Apparently, she was really scared.'

'Oh God, I didn't even think of that!'

'I kept an eye on her from the window,' Rahul reassured her. 'And I called Sam to pick her up. He was there in twenty minutes.'

'But I still forgot about her,' said Paddy, guilt-stricken. 'God, *she* would never have done that to me, no matter how angry she was.'

Rahul couldn't argue with that. 'Don't worry,' he reassured her. 'Sam will make her see sense and everything will be fine.'

But Padmini shook her head, unconvinced. Rahul sat beside her, hoping against hope that it wasn't too late to fix this.

When Aastha woke up, she found herself in Sameer's bed, wrapped securely in his favourite quilt. She felt a familiar stirring of desire and affection for him, until the memory of the previous night came back to her and she remembered why she was at his house. A leaden sensation descended on her as she replayed the words she and Paddy had exchanged.

She sat up slowly and spotted the mattress on the floor. She realized guiltily that Sameer had spent the night there, though he had been with her on the bed when she had cried herself to sleep.

Sighing, she made her way to the living room. Sameer was sitting on the couch, looking unusually pensive. 'Hey,' she said.

'Hey,' he replied. 'How are you, now?'

He waved the question away, and fixed her with a serious look. 'So, we need to talk.'

'That sounds rather ominous,' she said.

'It's not,' he said. 'But it could take a while, so let's have breakfast first.'

'What're you offering?' she asked, trying to ignore the flutter of anxiety in her stomach.

'Eggs, Quaker oats, Chocos, baked beans and pancakes.'

'What are you, a breakfast buffet?' she asked, momentarily amused. He was such a spoilt rich kid, sometimes. 'Who the hell has *baked beans* in their fridge?'

'Not everyone can get by on brown bread every single morning,' he retorted.

'I'll have Chocos,' she said.

He disappeared into the kitchen and emerged a few minutes later, carrying two bowls of cereal. They ate quickly and silently, until Aastha's curiosity finally got the better of her. 'What did you want to talk about?' she asked.

'I know things have been weird between us lately,' he said, 'but I want to forget all that for now. I still consider you one of my closest friends and I'm going to be completely frank.'

'You know you can say anything to me,' she said, saddened that he felt the need to ask for permission. 'A lot of things might have changed between us, but that hasn't.'

He looked relieved and then his expression grew serious again. 'I spoke to Rahul and he told me what happened. You really crossed the line.'

She bristled. 'You weren't even there! I don't know what he told you, but—'

'He told me you weren't there, either,' Sameer said, his voice hard. 'You just jumped to conclusions. Paddy hit him first. He tried to stop her and his hand got knocked against her eye by mistake.'

'You seriously believe that?' she asked, disgusted. 'What a lame excuse!'

'It's not an excuse,' Sameer said. 'Even if I hadn't spent so much time with him over the last couple of months, I would have known he was incapable of hitting someone. The fact that you're so convinced he did, tells me how blind and judgemental you've become.'

He had never spoken to her so harshly before and it hurt. 'You didn't see the state Paddy was in after they broke up,' she tried to defend herself. 'She cried all the time, she barely ate anything and she kept throwing up. Rahul isn't *good* for her and he's only going to hurt her again.'

'You are too involved in her love life,' said Sameer severely. 'Just because you were there for her when she needed you doesn't mean you get to dictate her entire relationship!'

'I *don't* dictate—!'

'Yeah, you do,' said Sameer, unrelenting. 'How many times have you given advice when she didn't ask for it? You did that with me and Karuna, too.'

'I didn't exactly hear you complain,' she said, hurt and offended. 'In fact, aren't you the one who kept pushing me to tell you what I thought about you getting married?'

'The difference is, you actually like Karuna,' said Sameer, 'which is why you gave me good advice. Yes, there were times when the nosiness annoyed me, but I sort of got used to it; even came to rely on it. You always made sense when you spoke to me.'

Aastha tried to ignore the sting of prickling discomfort at his use of the word 'nosiness'. 'Well, if I make so much sense, then why won't Paddy listen to me?' she demanded.

'God, why do you always have to be so stubborn?' Sameer groaned, frustrated. 'You don't give Paddy enough credit. She can manage her own relationship without your help!'

'Why should I give her any credit?' she shot back. 'And besides, Paddy threw me out of the house in the middle of the night! Neither of them even bothered to check if I was okay.'

'Rahul did,' said Sameer. 'He called me as soon as you left, and he stayed at the window and kept an eye on you till I got there.'

Aastha was so stunned that she forgot her anger. 'He . . . he did?' she asked, faltering. That didn't sound at all like the Rahul she knew, but she also knew that Sameer wouldn't lie. Sameer *had* gotten there a lot faster than she had expected.

'I was still furious with him, because it really wasn't safe,' said Sameer carefully. 'But he felt really bad about leaving you there.'

She winced, because that *did* sound like the Rahul she knew. He always apologized the moment he knew he was in the wrong. She remembered, even though she didn't want to, how he had told Paddy immediately after he had cheated and not tried to lie or justify himself, as so many others would have done. Even though she wanted to hate him, she couldn't help but be touched that he'd stayed at the window to keep an eye on her.

'I think you owe him one hell of an apology,' said Sameer quietly.

The words made her defensive again. 'He still hit her,' she said, but it was lacking in conviction.

'You don't seriously believe that,' Sameer said.

She dropped her gaze.

'I've been spending a lot of time with him lately,' he continued softly. 'He was miserable the entire time they were apart. He had no illusions about how badly he had fucked up and he wasn't sure she'd ever give him another chance. Now that she has, he loves her far too much to risk hurting her again. And come on, you've known him for . . . how many years? Do you really think he could ever hit her?'

There was too much truth in Sameer's words. She tried to reconcile the Rahul that Sameer was describing with the abusive asshole she had built up in her head and found that she couldn't. And the last of her stubborn convictions shattered, leaving her feeling hollow and guilt-stricken.

'Am I really nosy?' she asked in a small voice.

'Yeah, you are,' said Sameer. 'But only with the people you really love. You do it because you're overprotective and loyal, which is probably why we've overlooked it for so long. But being protective isn't the same as telling someone what to do, you know?'

The words hit home. 'I'm sorry,' she said, blinking back tears. 'If I ever overstepped the line—I mean, with Karuna—'

'Don't apologize for that,' he interrupted. 'I already told you I appreciated your advice. The people you need to apologize to are Paddy and Rahul.'

'Yeah,' she said, morosely.

She thought about Rahul and the awful things she had said to him; the way she had compared Paddy to an abused wife. She felt deeply ashamed.

'I don't know if they'll ever forgive me,' she muttered.

'Of course they will,' said Sameer. 'That's what friends are for.'

She got up, feeling bolstered. 'I'd better do it now, then,' she said resolutely.

He smiled at her approvingly, looking profoundly relieved that his lecture had worked.

Half an hour later, she walked back into the room with a heart that felt several kilos lighter. 'Done,' she announced to Sameer with a relieved smile.

'What did you say, exactly?' he asked.

'That I was sorry and that I had no right to say the things I said. I promised to stop interfering in their relationship. Rahul was really nice about it, though he seemed bothered by the fact that I thought he was abusive. I said I was sorry for misjudging him, and that I wanted to try and get to know him better, and he said he would like that, too.'

'And Paddy?' Sameer asked.

Aastha laughed ruefully. 'She wouldn't even let me apologize. She was feeling really guilty that she chucked me out of the house—said it was unforgivable. I told her that the things I had said were pretty unforgivable, too, so we could call it even. I think it'll be a while before any of us can forget it completely, but we'll get there.'

'I told you they'd forgive you!' Sameer was smiling widely.

'All thanks to you,' she said gratefully. 'I really needed to hear that stuff and I know it couldn't have been easy for you.'

'Yeah, well, thank you for listening to me,' he replied. 'I honestly wasn't sure if I'd be able to convince you.'

'What do you mean?' she said, a little hurt. 'I'm not so stubborn that I can't admit when I'm wrong.'

'No, no,' he hastened to reassure her. 'I just wasn't sure

how receptive you'd be with the way things have been between us lately.'

'You're still my best friend, Sam,' she said. 'Who else was I going to listen to but you?'

He looked doubtful. 'Even after I fucked things up so badly?'

'That was an honest mistake,' she said. 'It was my fault for making it such a big deal.'

'It was a big deal,' he said. 'You waited fifteen minutes to call me last night. There was a time when you wouldn't have hesitated for a second.'

'That isn't on you,' she said, shaken. 'I'm the one who let things—' She faltered, not wanting to mention her feelings for him. 'You *tried* to reach out after that night; you *tried* to talk to me. I was the one who didn't—'

'Don't you dare turn this around on yourself,' he interrupted fiercely. 'You called me after I broke up with Karuna and all I did was bite your head off. I hate myself enough for what I put you through that night, without adding your self-blame to it. God, you must have been so terrified, waking up like that—'

'Wait, what?' she asked. 'What the hell are you talking about?'

'Don't play dumb,' he said. 'I know how badly it affected you, even though you tried to hide it. I know you hate it when people come up behind you and I was practically . . .' He cut the words off, his face colouring. 'It must have been just like the attack. No wonder you couldn't stand it when I touched you after that.'

Oh, fuck! He actually thought . . .

'Sameer,' she said urgently. 'You've got this all wrong, okay? I'm not traumatized. That *wasn't* the reason I acted so—'

The words froze abruptly as another realization hit her. Sameer had no clue how she felt about him. She couldn't tell him the truth, not now. After last night, she had realized that what she had missed most was his friendship. She could live with unrequited feelings if she could have that back. If she told him how she felt, she would ruin every chance she had of regaining their old equation.

He smiled sadly, as if her silence had confirmed his worst fears. 'It's fine, Aastha,' he said gently. 'I'm a big boy, I can face up to my own mistakes.'

'Sam, you can't blame yourself for this,' she said desperately. 'I *wasn't* affected, I really wasn't. I hugged you last night, didn't I? I wouldn't have done that if you'd really done something to hurt me.'

'I'm glad you decided to forgive me,' he said. 'But please don't try to excuse what I did.'

'I'm not trying to excuse anything,' she said, increasingly upset. 'You're my best friend and I *swear*, you've never let me down.'

'Stop lying to me, okay?' he said, his voice tight. 'Can we just drop it now?'

She stared at him, feeling completely helpless as she realized that there was no way to convince him without telling him the truth. The problem was, she wasn't sure she was ready to do that.

TWENTY-EIGHT

Karuna had expected that everything about her life would change after Joseph's family made the proposal. But after the first flurry of congratulatory phone calls from her relatives, everything went back to normal.

She still spent all her time studying, except for her meetings with Joseph. She and Joseph still had the same kind of conversations they had always had, except that now, sometimes, they also talked about things like living arrangements and buying furniture. Although she was still miserable about Sameer, she gradually began to make peace with her fate. As she came to know Joseph better, she became more comfortable with the thought of being married to him.

Her parents had set the engagement date for February, and had decided the wedding would be some time in July. That was only six months away, which caused her some panic. But once she'd had time to get used to the idea, she accepted that, too.

In her darker moments, she wondered when she had become such a doormat, making peace with everything her parents were forcing on her. But she tried not to think about that too much, since it only made her feel bitter. It was better for her and for Joseph that she just live with this now, and try to be happy with it.

And then suddenly, a week before the engagement was scheduled to happen, there was a call from Joseph's father on the landline number. He said he wanted to speak to her father and, thinking nothing of it, she passed the phone to him and went to her room.

An hour later, her parents came to her bedroom with uncharacteristically sombre expressions.

'What is it?' she asked, alarmed.

'We just got a phone call from Joseph's parents,' her mother said in a shaky voice. 'They're calling off the engagement.'

Karuna blinked at her uncomprehendingly. 'What?'

'They wouldn't say why, but we made a few phone calls,' her father continued. 'Apparently, Joseph has eloped with his high-school girlfriend. That too, a Hindu!' He shook his head, looking disgusted and disappointed. 'Good for nothing, ungrateful boy. Apparently, his whole family is in a state of shock—they never even suspected the two were still friends. How could they not know what was happening under their own roof? What terrible parents!'

Karuna stared at her father. Her heart was pounding. 'The wedding's off?' she asked shakily.

Her mother nodded, teary-eyed. 'He was such a good match for you,' she lamented.

Karuna couldn't speak. A tidal wave of relief swept over her, so intense that her eyes flooded with tears. She buried her face in her hands, barely hearing her parents' distressed exclamations. She was free. In that moment, she realized that she had never been ready for marriage at all, no matter how many times she'd told herself to accept it.

She felt her mother's hand stroking her hair, murmuring soothingly. It was a while before she registered what she was saying, but when she did, Karuna's blood ran cold. 'Don't worry, sweetheart. There are plenty of others. We'll start looking again and we'll find you someone just as good.'

She raised her head, staring at her parents incredulously. 'Are you seriously already talking about the next match? It hasn't even been a *minute* since you told me the wedding is off.'

'We can understand that you're upset about this,' her father said. 'But that doesn't mean we should give up hope. Obviously, it can't happen overnight, but once the scandal dies down, we'll start looking again.'

'We'll find you someone even better, you'll see,' her mother chimed in.

She took in her parents' implacable expressions and an awful consuming fury descended on her. They really only cared about marrying her off; nothing else mattered to them. After spending so long pushing her towards Joseph, they were coldly and pragmatically washing their hands of him, moving on to the next customer, as if this were a business deal.

'I need to be alone for a while,' she said.

Her father nodded. Her mother patted her head one last time, and they both left the room.

———

Two days later, she saw Joseph's name flashing on the screen of her phone. For the first time, she felt the stirrings of anger.

She had been completely prepared to spend the rest of her *life* with this guy, and he had obviously been lying to her from the beginning. For a moment, she considered not picking up the phone, but curiosity got the better of her as she wondered what he could possibly have to say to her.

'Hello?'

'Karuna,' said Joseph, sounding relieved. 'I wasn't sure you'd answer.'

'I almost didn't,' she said. 'What do you want?'

'Just to apologize,' he said. 'I know I probably hurt and embarrassed you and your family. I wanted to explain.'

'Explain what?' she asked angrily. 'How well you had everyone fooled?'

'I never meant to lie to you,' he said. 'Tanya and I *did* break up after high school, and she did go to the UK to study. We stayed in touch, but we weren't together. I don't think either of us really got over each other, though. She came back to Bangalore a year ago and I started meeting her again. We weren't dating officially, not at the beginning, but it sort of spiralled out of control. Then my parents started talking about marriage and, well, they would never have accepted her. She's Hindu. She begged me to say no, said she was even willing to elope, but I didn't want to disappoint my parents. But I was still in love with her. The closer we got to the engagement, the more I panicked. A few days ago, I couldn't take it any more. So I called her and we eloped.'

Karuna didn't know what to think. The story had hit a little too close to home. Even though she wanted to stay angry with him, she couldn't. 'I . . . I guess that makes sense,' she said reluctantly. 'Actually, I haven't been completely honest with you, either.'

'What are you talking about?'

'Remember I told you about Sameer?' she said.

'You said you broke up with him less than a year ago,' Joseph responded.

'It was three months ago,' said Karuna. 'I was still seeing him while we were speaking on the phone. We were together for five years, but he wasn't ready to marry me, so I broke up with him.'

'Huh,' he said, surprised. 'It's almost exactly the same thing.'

'No, it's not,' said Karuna, bitterly. 'You get your happy ending, at least. I'm just stuck here. My parents are already talking about finding another match. I don't think they've even called the caterers to cancel the food for our engagement party, and they've moved on. I was so fucking relieved when I found out the engagement was off, but it's not like they're going to give me a break. If I tell them I can't do this again, it won't matter to them.'

'If you can't do it, then don't,' said Joseph forcefully. 'Get out while you still can. It's not worth it. Yeah, my parents are crushed. My mom called me and cried for an hour, and my dad won't even speak to me. They're probably never going to forgive me for this and that's fucking awful. But at the same time, I'm also so relieved. So happy that I had the guts to do this, because Tanya's worth it.'

'It's not that easy,' said Karuna. 'They wouldn't listen to me if I said no—I would have to get out of Bangalore before they could understand I'm serious. I'd have to find a job and go to Delhi; I don't even have any money saved for a flight ticket—'

'You'd get a job easily with your qualifications,' Joseph

interrupted. 'As for the money, I can lend you some if you need it. I have enough saved.'

She bristled. 'Do you seriously think I have no pride—?'

'Screw your pride,' Joseph interrupted fiercely. 'If you don't want my help, ask your friends, ask your cousins, ask anyone who'd be willing to help you. You can even sell the jewellery my family gave you, for all I care. Just get out while you still can. You have no idea how liberating it is. I felt so trapped before . . . and now it's like I can finally breathe.'

'I'll have to think about this,' she said, feeling lost.

'Then do that,' he said. 'But I meant what I said about helping you. I feel like we've become good friends over the last few months and I don't want to completely lose touch with you.'

'Wouldn't Tanya have a problem with you talking to me?'

'No, she'll understand,' he said. 'I never had feelings for you and she knows that. Just remember that it's your life, your future. Are you really willing to sacrifice it for your parents?'

He hung up on her before she had a chance to respond.

The next few days were the most agonizing ones of her life. She didn't even try to study and spent hours together pacing around her room.

More than once, she felt the urge to call Sameer, to ask if he would take her back if she moved to Delhi, but she forced herself not to. This decision had to be hers alone; she couldn't do this for him or anyone else.

One day, she overheard her mother talking to her aunt on the phone. 'No, it isn't as bad as we thought it was,' she was saying. 'I think everyone knows the engagement broke because of him, not because of any problem with *our* daughter.

I spoke to Shilpa Chechi the other day, she was talking about her second cousin's son—apparently, they are looking for a girl for him. She said he would be coming to Bangalore in two or three months, so we can introduce him then. He is an architect, lives in Mysore.'

Sick at heart, Karuna slipped back into her room. This was even worse.

She realized, with sudden, sharp clarity, that she couldn't go through with it. She had been fortunate once, being spared something she was nowhere near ready for, but it wouldn't happen a second time. She had to find herself a job and get out of the city. The obvious choice was Delhi, since many of her friends were there, and she would need all the support she could get once she walked away from her family.

Once her mind was made up, she logged on to a job portal and began to look for positions she could apply for. There were a few openings that fit her qualifications. She sent her résumé to them, but knew she wouldn't hear back for a few weeks—these things always took time. Still, even taking that first step made her feel more in control of her life than she had in ages.

The second step was to call Padmini and tell her what she had decided. She timed her phone call late in the evening, after her friend's office hours, and she picked up immediately. 'Hey, Karuna, how are you?'

'Fine,' she replied. 'I guess you heard about the engagement?'

'Yeah, I did,' said Padmini cautiously. 'I figured you needed space, though. Are you okay?'

'I was so fucking relieved,' she confessed. 'I didn't want to marry him; I was an idiot to have agreed. But unfortunately, my parents are already looking for someone else. I know they'll bully me into another match if I stay here, and I can't do it again. I want to move to Delhi.'

'I am so, so happy to hear you say that,' said Padmini fervently. 'Do you need help? You should talk to your college friends and ask them if there are vacancies in their companies, and I'll ask Rahul to recommend you in his company, too. Maybe you could even replace him; your job profiles are pretty similar. He's giving in his notice next week, as soon as his new job offer gets finalized.'

'He's quitting?' Karuna asked, side-tracked momentarily. 'You must be so relieved.'

'You have no idea,' said Padmini. 'But yeah, about you. What can I do to help? Do you need money? I don't have much saved, but we'll figure something out. And obviously, you'll stay with me till you get on your feet.'

'Thanks, Paddy,' said Karuna, touched. 'I might decide to take you up on that, but first, I have to at least get a few calls for job interviews. I have a couple of months before my parents get on my case again, and I'm going to spend the time searching and hoping something comes up.'

'I'm sure it will work out,' Padmini said. 'Even if it doesn't, you can still move here if things get really bad, and we can figure out the rest later.'

'Thanks,' Karuna repeated.

'Any time. I have to go now; we're having Game Night and everyone just got here. I'll talk to you later, okay? I'm *so* proud of you.'

She hung up, leaving Karuna feeling both sad and hopeful. She knew it was practical to wait before rushing off to Delhi without a job in hand, but that wasn't the only reason she didn't want to go immediately. She knew these were the last few weeks she would enjoy being on good terms with her parents, and she didn't want them to end.

It made her heart ache when she thought of how devastated her parents would be when she left.

She knew going to Delhi wouldn't end their attempts at marrying her off. They would keep trying when a good match came their way. They would call her up, and plead with her, and she would end up ignoring their calls out of sheer frustration. Going to Delhi would be the start of a long bitter period full of arguments and tears. Eventually, she hoped, she would be able to bridge the distance between them. But it wouldn't be for a long, long time.

Are you sure your family won't want the jewellery back? It's worth quite a bit.

I'm sure. They'd be too embarrassed to ask for it again. Does this mean you're getting out, then?

Got a couple of job interviews lined up in Delhi. I wish I didn't have to use it, it feels like I'm cheating, somehow.

It was a gift, so it's yours now. You can do whatever the hell you want with it. Let me know when you land in Delhi, so Tanya and I can toast your release from jail. I am so, so happy for you.

'Amma, Appa, I need to talk to you about something,' Karuna said. Her parents exchanged concerned looks.

'I want to go and work in Delhi,' Karuna said before they could ask.

'You'll do no such thing,' her father stated, his eyes hard.

'I'm not asking you,' Karuna said, meeting his gaze squarely. 'I've got three job interviews in Delhi next week and I know I'll get one of them. I've already booked the tickets. I'm leaving this Sunday.'

Sunday was only four days away, her mother thought, shell-shocked. How had this happened?

'What! How could you go and do this without asking us?' her father exclaimed. 'Why this sudden need to go to Delhi and work?'

'It's not sudden,' said Karuna. 'I don't want to get married and if I stay here, you guys will keep trying to force me into it.'

'No one is forcing you—' her father began.

'I know about that boy from Mysore,' she interrupted, and her mother started with surprise. 'When were you going to tell me about that, by the way? After you'd already decided everything?' She shook her head in disgust. 'I can't do this again.'

'Sweetheart,' her mother pleaded with her. 'We're only doing this for your own good. As your parents, we—'

'I've heard all that before,' said Karuna. 'I love you both, but you need to understand that this is *my* life, *my* future. I almost let you marry me off to someone I had no feelings for. I was absolutely miserable, but you didn't even care! And now you're all set to try again, without bothering to ask how I feel about it. I can't stay here any more.'

'If you leave, we'll cut you off,' said her father, his voice stony. 'No money, no help, you're completely on your own. We won't even pay for your coaching classes.'

Her mother flinched at his words, but Karuna didn't even look surprised. 'I knew you would say that,' she muttered. 'But did you miss the part where I said I had three job interviews? I don't need your money.' She turned on her heel and walked out of the room.

Her mother felt as if her world was coming down around her ears. She rushed after her daughter. 'Karuna, please, why are you doing this? Is it because of that boy? I don't understand why you can't just—'

'This has nothing to do with Sameer,' said Karuna. 'And I know you don't understand. If you did, I wouldn't have had to do this.' She smiled sadly. 'Don't try to stop me.'

She walked away.

TWENTY-NINE

Things were finally getting back to normal within their group. Aastha had made up with Padmini completely, and nothing had really changed between them. Not that she had expected it to. Even when she'd been screaming her lungs out at Paddy, she'd known it wasn't the end of their friendship.

Aastha also began to make a conscious effort to get to know Rahul better. The more she observed him with Paddy, the more she realized that she'd misjudged him. It was obvious that he was madly in love with her and was genuinely sorry for hurting her.

Something had changed between them. They still had nasty arguments every now and then, still said hurtful things to each other, but they also let things go and forgave each other with a lot less fuss than they used to. It was as if they had grown up, somehow. Aastha tried to follow their example and bit her tongue whenever she wanted to give them advice or interfere.

As for Sameer, after their conversation, it was as if the air had cleared between them. He teamed up with her on Game Nights, just like the old days, teased her good-naturedly, texted her from work, and generally behaved just like the old Sameer. But he still wouldn't touch her.

Now that she knew the real reason for his hesitation, it tormented her. The idea that he believed he had traumatized her in some way was unbearable. She wanted to shake him by the shoulders and scream at him until he believed it wasn't his fault. But of course, he wouldn't believe her unless she told him the truth. More and more, she found herself struggling with the desire to just tell him and get it over with. Perhaps it would damage their friendship again, but wasn't it unfair to let him blame himself?

Her inner turmoil was pushed to the brink during one Game Night, when she was standing in her kitchen making Maggi for her friends. She was so absorbed in her thoughts that she didn't even hear Sameer come in, until his voice sounded from directly behind her. 'How's it coming? I'm hungry.'

She started badly, dropping the wooden spoon she was stirring with. 'Shit!' she cursed.

'Dude,' said Rahul who was leaning against the kitchen doorway. 'You sure scare easy.'

'Sorry,' Sameer said, backing away from her. 'We just came to give you company. I shouldn't have come up behind you.'

'Sam, no,' she protested forcefully. 'It wasn't—honestly, I was just startled—'

'*Don't*,' said Sameer. 'Just . . . don't make excuses.'

He turned and walked past Rahul into the living room.

'What the hell was that about?' Rahul asked.

'Nothing important,' she mumbled.

'I thought you and Sameer were okay now.'

She was so shocked that she nearly dropped the spoon again. 'He told you?!'

'Nothing in detail!' he hastened to reassure her, visibly alarmed by her reaction. 'I noticed you guys seemed off and I asked him about it. He said he made a mistake which really hurt you and that things between you became awkward. But lately, you seemed pretty much back to normal. I honestly thought you'd managed to fix things.'

'He didn't do anything,' she said, increasingly upset. 'He keeps blaming himself, but it wasn't his fault at all! I mean, I guess it was, but it was an accident, and I didn't even get affected that badly—I mean I did, but not in the way he thinks—'

'Dude, seriously, you're not making *any* sense,' Rahul interrupted, his eyes wide. 'Take a breath and start at the beginning. And by the way, I think the Maggi's done.'

She turned the stove off and began to rifle through the cupboards for bowls, using the distraction to cover her confusion. She had never actually confided in Rahul before and this was something she didn't want even Padmini to know about.

As if reading her mind, Rahul said, 'I won't tell Paddy, if that's what you're worried about.'

She straightened, four plastic bowls clutched in her hand. 'I—it's not that I don't trust her,' she stammered. 'I'm just afraid of how she'd react. I don't want her to overanalyse it, or—'

'You don't need to explain,' said Rahul. 'You have a right to tell whomever you want. If you don't want to tell me, that's fine, too, but you're obviously really upset, and I already know something, anyway. So I'm here if you want to talk.'

She had promised to give Rahul a chance, to become better friends with him, and now it was her turn to prove that she'd meant it. Taking a deep breath, she began, 'I, uh, can't tell you the details. But basically, something happened in Goa which made me realize I had feelings for Sameer.'

Rahul didn't even blink. 'I knew it,' he muttered to himself.

'You did?' she asked, surprised and dismayed. 'Was I that obvious?'

'No,' said Rahul. 'But it just made sense, with how you both were behaving. So that's why things got messed up between you two, because he found out you liked him?'

'I *thought* that was the reason,' Aastha replied, 'but it turns out he has no clue that I like him. He thought he hurt me, really hurt me, and that was why I was acting so distant. But that wasn't the reason at all! I just couldn't deal with my feelings. But now, every time I tell him it wasn't his fault, he thinks I'm just trying to sugarcoat things and refuses to believe me.'

'Wow,' said Rahul. 'That's really . . . complicated.'

'I know.' She sighed. 'I don't know what to do. It's not fair to him to let him keep feeling guilty for something he didn't do. But if I tell him I have feelings for him, I'm scared it'll ruin our friendship for good.'

'It won't,' said Rahul. 'You guys are too close for him to ever turn his back on you, no matter what. I think you should tell him, especially now that he and Karuna have broken up.'

Aastha stiffened in surprise. 'I *really* don't think he's going to return my feelings, even without her in the picture,' she said.

'I didn't mean that,' he said. 'But it'll be a lot easier to tell him if he's single.'

She thought about this for a long moment. 'You really think I should tell him?'

'I think for someone as principled as you, you wouldn't be able to live with yourself if you didn't,' said Rahul. 'Besides,' he continued, 'I don't think it's fair to let him feel guilty for something he didn't do.'

'Yeah, I know it isn't,' she muttered.

Now that Rahul had pointed it out, she knew she would have to tell him. Just the fact that she had made a decision made her feel better. She grabbed two bowls of Maggi and headed for the living room, pausing briefly to glance back at him. 'Hey, thanks, Rahul.'

'Any time.'

———

But Aastha's plans of telling Sameer the truth were derailed by an unforeseen development. The four friends were eating dinner at a restaurant when Padmini's cell phone buzzed. She reached for it, swiping her thumb across the screen to read the text message.

Her eyes grew wide and she jumped up and hurried out of the restaurant. Sameer, Aastha and Rahul exchanged confused looks. They could see Paddy through the glass doors, talking animatedly with someone on the phone.

When she came back a few minutes later, she had a strange expression on her face.

'Everything okay?' Sameer asked.

'I'm not sure,' Padmini said cautiously. 'It depends.'

'On what?' he asked, frowning.

'On how you react,' she said. 'I just got a call from one of my friends in Bangalore. She told me Karuna's engagement broke off yesterday.'

Sameer's face lit up with hope, and Aastha's heart sank.

'I knew she would come to her senses,' he breathed.

Padmini winced, obviously realizing he had misunderstood. 'Um, no,' she said. 'It wasn't her idea to break the engagement off, it was Joseph's. Apparently, he was already in love with someone else and he eloped with her. It was completely out of the blue.'

Sameer's face fell. 'How do you know?' he asked.

'It's a big scandal for everyone who knows the family,' Padmini said. 'Everyone's gossiping about it. My friend found out through some relative whose maid's sister works in his family.'

'So—it wasn't her decision, then,' he muttered, looking disappointed and hurt.

He didn't say anything for a long moment, and then, abruptly, he rose and strode out of the restaurant. Aastha hesitated only a moment before she jumped up to follow him. She pursued him at a safe distance, not entirely sure that he would welcome her presence.

Sameer walked until he came to a secluded corner and sank down on one of the steel benches that lined the walls. Aastha approached him hesitantly. 'If you want me to leave you alone, I will.'

'No, it's fine,' he said, and she sat down beside him.

She tried to think of what to say to him, but found herself hesitating. The reasons she had avoided talking about Karuna were still very much present, and she couldn't deny that deep down, she didn't want him to get back together with her. But he obviously needed to talk, or he wouldn't have asked her to sit down and she didn't want to fail him again. 'I know you're disappointed that this wasn't her decision,' she said carefully. 'But it does mean she's single again. Are you thinking of getting back together with her?'

'I don't know,' he said. 'I really miss her, but it really screwed with my head when she said yes to Joseph. One month after our break-up, and she was all ready to move on? If he hadn't run away, she'd still be marrying him.'

'I know you're hurt, but you shouldn't write her off completely,' said Aastha. 'You both have a lot of history. You should probably try to talk about this, figure things out.'

'Yeah,' he said, and then after a pause, 'we should probably head back.'

They retraced their steps and rejoined the other two. Even though they all made an effort to keep the mood light, Sameer was quiet and distant for most of the meal. No one was surprised when he headed back home instead of joining them as he had planned.

Aastha was feeling quite low by the time Rahul drove them back to her house. Rahul must have noticed, because he asked in an undertone, 'You okay?'

'Fine,' she said, not very convincingly.

'I know this probably sucks for you,' he said sympathetically. 'But if you were planning to, I don't think now is the time to tell him anything about your feelings.'

'Of course not,' she responded immediately. 'He's already going through enough without me adding to it.'

As they reached the house, Rahul squeezed her shoulder

reassuringly. 'Don't worry so much. I'm sure all of this is going to work out soon.'

'Yeah,' she said with a grateful smile. 'Thanks.'

It was only later that she realized that he had been behind her when he squeezed her shoulder, and yet she hadn't even noticed at the time.

———

Karuna nearly cried when she remembered her parents' faces as her cab had pulled out of the driveway. But she had to be firm.

Delhi airport was a bustling, busy place, and she felt very small and insignificant as she pushed her loaded trolley towards the exit. The sunlight outside was dazzling, making her screw her eyes shut.

When she opened them again, she saw Padmini and Rahul standing right in front of her.

Her face crumpled and she threw her arms around her friend. 'It's okay, you're okay,' Padmini murmured. 'Everything's going to be fine, you'll see. Shall we head home now?'

Home.

She had just left it behind, probably for good. But Delhi was her home, too. Her closest friends were here, her job, her freedom. No one here would try to force her to do anything she didn't want to. She could live her life on her own terms. The thought filled her with newfound fortitude and, for the first time since she had left home, she smiled.

'Yeah,' she said. 'Let's go home.'

THIRTY

The news that Karuna's engagement was off put Sameer in a tailspin. He hadn't realized until then how much he'd been hoping she would come back to him. Perhaps he should be happy that she wasn't getting married, but it hadn't been her choice. He found that that one fact changed everything.

Of course, he had no idea whether she even wanted to get back with him. She had not called him even once and it was only through Padmini that he had found out she was back in Delhi. It was what they had always wanted during the long-distance phase of their relationship—for her to be in the same city so they could meet each other more often. But now, he didn't know how to react to the news.

The fact that she was now living in Paddy's house made things a little awkward. They couldn't have Game Nights at her place any more; it was now invariably at Aastha's house. Paddy made a big effort not to let her friendship with Sameer suffer because of her new house guest, but she did have to divide her time between the two, and sometimes she and Rahul would leave early after Game Night, or cancel on them for dinner because they had to spend time with Karuna, too.

These were minor changes, however, and they didn't upset Sameer. He was glad that Karuna had good friends in Delhi to help her at such a difficult time. About a month after she had moved back she called him.

'Hey, Karuna,' he greeted her.

'Hey,' she replied, 'I'm, uh, sorry it took me so long to call. I know we have things we need to talk about, but I was in the middle of a bunch of job interviews and I couldn't afford the distraction.'

'I understand,' he said. 'Did you crack the interviews?'

'Rahul's old company is calling me for their HR round tomorrow,' she said. 'It's the last round, so I'm probably going to get it; just have to negotiate the salary.'

'That's great!' he said with genuine warmth. 'You must be so relieved.'

'You have no idea,' she said. There was a short pause and then she added cautiously, 'So I think we should probably meet. Our last conversation didn't exactly end on an amazing note, and a lot's happened since then that we should probably talk about. Besides, I haven't seen you in so long—it doesn't feel right that I've been here this long and haven't even met you yet.'

'Yeah, I know what you mean,' he said. 'My place?'

'Yeah,' she said, sounding relieved. 'Unless you just want to do lunch, or something?'

'No,' he said immediately. The conversation would probably be an emotional one and he didn't want to have it in a public place.

'Okay, cool.'

They scheduled the meeting for the coming Saturday and Sameer spent the next few days agonizing about what he would say to her. He almost didn't go for Game Night on Friday, but Aastha insisted that he come. He was glad that he did, because it took his mind off things.

He drove back to his apartment the next day, promising to return to Aastha's house once his meeting was over. He knew he would probably need the distraction of his friends around him; he had a feeling the conversation wasn't going to end with them getting back together.

He spent half an hour tidying his flat, trying to work off his restlessness. When she rang the doorbell, he flung the door open. For a second, they both stood there, frozen, and then, though Sameer was never sure who had moved first, they were hugging each other tightly. He felt some of his anxiety slip away. This was still Karuna, after all, and no matter how this conversation turned out, she would always hold a special place in his heart.

Finally, they broke apart and Sameer ushered her to the living room sofa. They were both silent, and then Sameer cleared his throat. 'So, first of all, I'm sorry about the way I yelled at you when you told me you were getting engaged. I know I didn't handle that very well.'

'I understand why you reacted that way,' Karuna said. 'If the roles were reversed, I probably would have done the same. I don't know, maybe I shouldn't have told you like that, but I just didn't want you to hear it from anyone else.'

'No, that would have been awful,' he said. 'I'm glad you told me.'

'I don't know if I'm way off base here,' Karuna said

cautiously, 'but I've been thinking. I'm not engaged any more. I don't know if that means anything for the two of us.'

'I've been thinking about that too,' he said. 'I know it would make sense. You're in Delhi, your parents aren't in the picture any more, so all the reasons for which we broke up are pretty much non-existent.'

'But?' she prompted him, sensing from his tone that he wasn't finished.

'It really hurt me that you were willing to marry him,' said Sameer. 'I thought you'd come to your senses eventually, that you'd work up the nerve to say no, but you never did. The truth is, if he hadn't been the one to say no, you would probably be his fiancée right now.'

'You have no idea how glad I am it didn't come to that. I was completely miserable. Even with the engagement a week away, I couldn't stop thinking about you.'

'That only makes things worse,' he said. 'You were willing to marry someone while you were still in love with me. That's just . . . it really hurt me.'

She blinked back tears. 'You really hurt me, too. You weren't willing to commit to me when it counted.'

'It was unfair of you to expect that of me,' he said, with only a hint of anger.

'Was it?' she asked. 'If you really loved me, it shouldn't have been that hard.'

'I could say the same thing about you and Joseph,' he shot back.

They stared at each other, realizing they had reached an impasse. Each thought the other had wronged them and neither of them could let it go. There was no way to fix this and Sameer wasn't even sure he wanted to. He still loved her, but he had grown apart from her in the past few months and he could see that she had, too.

'So I guess that's it then,' he said sadly. 'I'm sorry.'

'It's probably for the best,' Karuna said, trying to smile. 'I have to build a life here; I have to earn and become independent and come to terms with the fact that I walked out on my parents. I should focus on that for now and not think about a relationship.'

'I'm really proud of you, by the way,' Sameer said. 'I know it wasn't easy for you to walk away. If you need any help, you can always come to me. For money or anything else.'

She shook her head. 'I appreciate it, but I don't think my pride could take that,' she said. 'Besides, I'm okay for now.'

'I'm still your friend, Karuna,' he said, a little hurt. 'Or at least, I hope I am.'

'Of course you are,' she hastened to reassure him, 'but it'll be a while before you're *just* that and I don't want to complicate things by asking you for help.' She took a deep breath. 'I don't think we should talk or meet again for a while. I know I said that last time, too, and we're both here, but I really mean it this time. If we keep meeting, I'll never get over you.'

He nodded, knowing she was right. It cut him deeply. 'I hope you meant it when you said you didn't want us to lose touch,' he said. 'You've been too huge a part of my life for too long and I can't picture you out of it completely.'

'I can't either,' she said. 'I don't think that's going to happen. Maybe it'll take a few years, but I hope we end up as really good friends.'

He nodded. For some reason, this felt a lot more final than their actual break-up had been. With a heavy heart, he hugged her goodbye, feeling as if a large chapter in his life had just drawn to a close.

THIRTY-ONE

Rahul watched Aastha with wary concern. She had been vibrating with tension for the entire time Sameer had been with Karuna. Rahul had stayed behind at Aastha's place, thinking she might need a friend, and he was glad he had done so, when, after trying to call Sameer, she handed him her cell phone.

'Don't give it back to me for a few hours,' she told him.

'Why?' he asked, confused by her actions.

'I don't want to be tempted to call him again. He obviously needs his space, and I'm trying not to be too pushy. He knows I'm here and he'll come over if he wants to.'

Rahul was impressed by her restraint. She was obviously trying very hard to turn over a new leaf. The fact that she'd trusted him with her feelings for Sameer had touched and surprised him. Slowly, they were actually becoming friends.

The doorbell rang and Aastha sprang up to open the door. She paused when she saw Sameer and then stood back to let him enter.

Sameer didn't say anything in response. Rahul caught sight of his bloodshot eyes and winced. Obviously, things with

Karuna hadn't ended well. Aastha seemed to know exactly what to do. Without saying a word, she tugged him towards the living room. She plugged her hard drive into the TV and played an episode of *Big Bang Theory*.

For a while, Sameer remained rigid with tension, but then slowly, as the sounds of studio laughter washed over him, he began to relax. Absently, he put an arm around Aastha, who was sitting next to him on the sofa. For a few moments, it seemed to Rahul as if all the tension between them had vanished, but then Sameer jerked his arm away as if he'd been burnt.

'Sorry,' he muttered.

Aastha's face fell. Sameer got up and walked towards the kitchen, leaving her staring at him with a stricken expression.

'This is ridiculous,' Rahul told her. 'You have to tell him the truth.'

'Now?' she asked, shocked. 'This is hardly the time to—'

'No,' Rahul interrupted. 'He really needs you right now, but he's obviously holding back. It's not fair that he's still blaming himself—he doesn't need that on top of everything else. You need to tell him it wasn't his fault.'

Aastha looked a little uncertain, but her expression cleared when Sameer came back, a plate full of buttered toast in his hand, and sat down on the opposite end of the sofa, as far away from her as he could get.

Aastha met Rahul's eyes and nodded once. He took his cue and left soon after that, hoping the two would manage to work things out in his absence.

Sameer could feel the weight of Aastha's eyes on his back. He shifted uncomfortably. She had been staring at him on and off for the last hour, an apprehensive, measuring look in her eyes.

'Just spit it out,' he said.

'W—what?' she stammered.

He gentled his tone. 'I can tell you have something you want to say to me,' he said. 'I don't know why you're afraid of my reaction, but—'

'No, no, it's not that,' she said, agitated. 'I'm just not sure this is the best time. I made up my mind that I had to tell you, but it might seem really insensitive for me to be saying it when you've just ended things with Karuna.'

He stared at her, his curiosity roused. 'What is it, Aastha?'

She jumped up from her beanbag and began to pace around the room. She was breathing in short quick puffs, almost panting, and he was disturbed to see that she actually looked afraid.

'Aastha, you're starting to scare me.'

'Don't say anything,' she said shakily. 'I'm trying to gather my nerve here and I'll lose it if you interrupt me.'

He watched her walking up and down in a perturbed silence, until she suddenly came to a stop right in front of him. 'So, first of all, I'm only telling you this because I don't want you to keep blaming yourself for what happened in Goa,' she said.

'Aastha,' he began. 'Please don't try to excuse—'

'I told you not to interrupt me,' she said tightly. 'Uh, when I woke up that night, I thought I was dreaming at first. I wasn't scared, not for a second. For the first time, a guy was holding me, and I felt safe and comfortable.' Her face had turned a bright red, and she refused to meet his eyes. 'For those few minutes, I felt loved. And then you said Karuna's name and it completely shattered the illusion that—' She took a deep breath.

Sameer stared at her with wide uncomprehending eyes. Whatever he'd been expecting, it hadn't been this.

'Anyway,' she said, her gaze fixed firmly on the floor. 'Once I saw you in that light, I couldn't un-see it. That's why I was so awkward around you. Every time you touched me, it reminded me of how I felt when you—' She cut herself off again and took a deep gasping breath.

'Yeah. So, I thought I'd made it really obvious, how I felt, and that's why you were so uncomfortable around me. I didn't know you thought you'd *traumatized* me. I can't believe you could ever think that. You're the person who stood by me during the darkest period of my life. I know what it feels like to be violated and I've *never* felt that way with you. And I know you're still in love with Karuna, and I don't expect anything from you. We can pretend this conversation never happened, if you want, but please stop blaming yourself, or acting as if I'll fall apart every time you touch me. I won't.'

She stopped talking and wrapped her arms around her middle, still refusing to meet his gaze. Sameer stared at her, completely speechless. He had no idea how to react.

'Please say something, Sam,' she said, when the silence grew too long.

'I . . .' he began, trailing off helplessly.

Her face crumpled and she began to turn away. Instinctively, he reached out and caught her hand. 'Don't,' he said. 'Just give me a second, okay? I'm not mad, I'm not freaked out; I just need a second to process this.'

She nodded slowly. He pulled her gently towards the sofa, and she followed his unspoken cue and sat down beside him. He retained his grip on her hand and forced himself to think about what she had said. When the shock wore off, his first emotion was intense relief. It was a weight off his shoulders to know that he hadn't hurt her.

Now that he thought about it, so many things about the last few months made sense. 'Is this why you wouldn't give me advice about Karuna?' he asked.

'Yeah,' she said softly. 'I didn't want to, you know, be biased.'

It spoke volumes that she hadn't trusted herself to be impartial. This wasn't some silly crush she would get over in a few months. But he wasn't freaked out. The strongest, most principled person he knew had told him she had feelings for him. That wasn't something to shy away from as if it were unwanted or awkward. He didn't know how he felt, but it wasn't *bad*.

'I really appreciate that you . . .' he began and then stopped. 'Hey, look at me.' She met his eyes reluctantly. 'I really appreciate that you told me,' he said. 'I know it couldn't have been easy, but it was the right thing to do.'

She nodded, but didn't relax. 'And I'm not weirded out,' he continued. 'Maybe I should be, but I actually feel *flattered* that someone I care about and admire so much could feel that way about me. It's, well, humbling, I guess.'

'I just want us to stay friends,' she said in a small voice. 'If we can just pretend this didn't happen—'

'I can't, Aastha,' he said gently. 'Frankly, I don't even want to. What are you scared of, that I'll be all strange and awkward around you, like before?'

She nodded.

'Well, I won't,' he said firmly. 'I don't know if I'll ever be able to return your feelings, but I can't say for sure I'll *never* feel the same way. All I know for sure is that you're my best friend, and that you're always going to be a part of my life, and that's all that really matters to me.'

Her eyes filled with profound relief. 'I'm so, so glad to hear you say that,' she said, squeezing his hand. 'What I missed the most over the last few months was being your friend. I want you to be able to touch me without worrying that I'll freak out, or talk to me about Karuna without worrying if I'm feeling hurt. I'll be fine, as long as *we're* fine. That's all I really care about.'

He was moved by her words and drew her into a fierce hug, one that she returned with equal fervour. He felt her heart slowing against his, even as his shoulder grew moist with what were probably tears of relief.

———

As she rested her head against his shoulder, Aastha felt at peace. She thought about everything that had happened over the past year, all the ups and downs she'd had. On the surface of it, very little had changed about her life. But she felt older and wiser than she had six months ago, almost as if she had grown up.

Sameer had surprised her with his maturity when she had confessed her feelings. She thought about Rahul and Paddy, and how far they had come; how sure they seemed of their future together.

She didn't know where the future would take her, but she knew in that moment that no matter what happened, no matter what life threw at her, as long as she had her friends by her side, she would find the strength to face it.

ACKNOWLEDGEMENTS

There are several people to whom I owe a debt of gratitude for their help and encouragement:

Ma, for all your support, and for joining Facebook for the sole purpose of promoting my novels.

Pa, for your support, marketing advice, and your sharp eyes which are better than any spellcheck.

Achala, for being the best friend, editor and proofreader a girl could ever ask for.

Adeeb, for being my brainstorming buddy and for coming up with the title of this book.

All the friends and family who gave me so much support for my first book, from writing reviews on Flipkart, to making time to attend my book discussions.

Vaishali Mathur, for signing me on in the first place and for continuing to have faith in my writing.

Arpita Basu, for editing my book and putting up with all my nitpicking over commas for a second time.